Charles Eugene Banks, Richard Hooker Wilmer, George Cram Cook

In Hampton Roads

A Dramatic Romance

Charles Eugene Banks, Richard Hooker Wilmer, George Cram Cook

In Hampton Roads
A Dramatic Romance

ISBN/EAN: 9783337347802

Printed in Europe, USA, Canada, Australia, Japan

Cover: Foto ©Andreas Hilbeck / pixelio.de

More available books at **www.hansebooks.com**

IN HAMPTON ROADS

A

DRAMATIC ROMANCE

BY

CHARLES EUGENE BANKS

AND

GEORGE CRAM COOK

CHICAGO AND NEW YORK:
RAND, McNALLY & COMPANY,
PUBLISHERS.

CONTENTS.

—

DRAMATIS PERSONÆ.

—

LIEUTENANT EARL HAMILTON, U. S. N., *stationed on the Frigate Minnesota.*

GEN. HUGO VON BENZINGER, U. S. A., *in command of a brigade stationed near Hampton Roads.*

CAPTAIN GEARY,
LIEUTENANT EDWARDS, } *of his staff.*

WATERLOO WILLIS, *of the Secret Service.*

CAPTAIN LAFE HARLAN, C. S. A., *commanding a company of guerrillas.*

SQUIRE HENDERSON, *a planter, in reduced circumstances.*

LITTLE JOE, *a dumb negro boy, property of the Squire.*

SETH, *an old negro servant of the Eggleston household.*

LIEUTENANT WORDEN, *commanding the Monitor.*

LIEUTENANT GREENE,
MR. STIMERS, } *of the Monitor.*
MR. WEBBER,

CAPTAIN BUCHANAN, *commanding the Merrimac.*

MAJOR CUTHBERTSON, *Brigade Surgeon, U. S. A.*

COLONEL MIDDLETON, U. S. A., *commanding a regiment at Camp Butler.*

CAPTAIN STANHOPE, U. S. A., *of Colonel Middleton's command.*

VIRGINIA EGGLESTON, *daughter of Judge Eggleston, of Waverley Plantation.*

MRS. CORA POYNTER, *her foster sister, of Washington, D. C.*

ESTELLE, *a white slave.*

BLACK MAMMIE, *of the Eggleston household.*

Soldiers, sailors, civilians, negroes, etc.

SCENES:—Waverley Plantation, overlooking Hampton Roads — Destruction of the Union fleet in Hampton Roads — On board the Monitor — Interior of Waverley.

TIME — March 8 and 9, 1862.

IN HAMPTON ROADS.

PROLOGUE.

THE BIRTII OF IRONCLADS.

Sumter had fallen. North and South had sprung
to arms. In Dixie and in Yankeeland thousands
had enlisted; regiment after regiment had been
massed, camped, clothed, drilled, equipped, organ-
ized and marched away. The unexhausted South
was pouring out her undiminished wealth. High
hope of victory sat on her banners, which shone
now with the luster of Manassas. For both sides,
however, war had changed from a romantic opportunity for glory to a grim and shattering reality.
Grant on the Mississippi was hammering at the
back door of the Confederacy. McClellan was
making a real army out of the disorganized and
routed thousands, who, in the previous June, had
blocked the roads to Washington. He had already

formed in his mind the idea of the peninsular campaign, which looked for its base of operations to Hampton Roads.   Here, at the mouth of the James, seventy miles below Richmond, was Fort Monroe—the cork of the Confederate bottle.

The Union troops, under Major General Wool, held the fort itself, the quaint old town of Hampton, and a strip of coast eight or ten miles long, extending across the southern extremity of the peninsula from the mouth of the York River to the mouth of the James, where, at Newport News Point, Federal batteries commanded the river.   Eight miles northwest of the fort, as the crow flies, were the Confederate outposts, whose main force, commanded by Magruder, lay from ten to twenty miles back in Yorktown and Williamsburg.   Confederate intrenchments and batteries at Big Bethel, Lee's Mill, Howard's Bridge, Warwick Courthouse and Ship's Point commanded every coigne of vantage on the northbound roads—the roads to Richmond.   The southeastern shore of Hampton Roads, the south bank of the James, the country lying all about Norfolk, was in the hands of the Confederates.   Their lines were unbroken from Richmond to the Sewall's Point batteries, which fronted, across three miles of blue water, the guns of Fort Monroe.   The waters of the great roadstead, where the warships lie, became in the early part of '62 the focus of the war, the point where the destinies of the widespread, mighty continent were to be decided.

This was the situation on Saturday morning, March eighth, eighteen hundred and sixty-two. The sun rose on an unclouded sky and shot arrows of silver along the peaceful waters of the great harbor, tipped with gold the masts of the Union frigates lying under the protecting guns of the fort, cast long shadows across the James River from the oaks that lined its banks, and between which lay the ships of the Confederate fleet waiting an opportunity to slip out to sea, and fell mellow and warm along the gently sloping hills of Old Virginia. Mating birds sang or chirruped in the crabapple trees, rich with blossoms and fragrant with perfume.

Back from the shore, upon the rising ground, groups of negroes armed with hoes moved lazily afield, chanting their musical, melancholy rhymes. Over toward Norfolk, fishermen dipped their oars in the placid waters, or drifted idly with the tide.

The morning was perfect. The ear of the listener heard no harsher sounds than those recounted; the eye saw no more disturbing sights. Occasionally the mellow notes of a distant bugle in routine call, the neighing of an impatient steed, or the droning cry of a weary sentinel suggested the nearness of armed and hostile forces—that was all. On this eventful morning the most important point of vantage to the arms of both the Federal and Confederate forces was as peaceful and serene as though the men in blue and the men in butternut, lying on their arms along each side of Hampton Roads, had been comrades in one cause as well as brothers in blood.

The same sun was to look down at noon upon this pastoral vale and quiet sea wrapped in the smoke of carnage and resounding with the roar of half a hundred batteries. It was to set upon a scene of desolation and death, of wreck-strewn waves dyed red with the blood of brave Americans, of sunken ships which carried with them into troubled waters the hopes of half the people of the most Christian nation of the earth.

It was the morning of the day in which a thought was to be tested; in which a new navy was to be born.

Today the Confederate ram, the Merrimac, the first ironclad ever tried, was to attack the Federal fleet. The sun looked on and made no sign.

CHAPTER I.

WAVERLEY PLANTATION.

Virginia Eggleston, standing on the gallery of Waverley mansion overlooking Hampton Roads on that memorable morning, felt something of the impending tragedy that was to be enacted there. Of the Merrimac she knew no more than others not in the secret of its building. Descriptions of this craft had been so many and conflicting that the imagination, quickened by the sweeping events of the time, could retain no more than their most striking features. These had gradually changed and shifted according to the mind or temperament of the individual, so that both at the North and the South the new ship was as mythical as the ancient dragon—all the more terrible because of the mystery surrounding it. To the Confederates it held out a hope for instant and lasting victory. To the Federals it was an undefined, intangible force, a wild beast, an animal of unknown dimensions, crouching for a spring. That a single ship could live for a moment in Hampton Roads, under the fire of the guns of the whole Union fleet and of the shore batteries, seemed no more than an idle boast. That such a craft could sink all those great ships and sail away unhurt to attack and burn the cities along the New England coast, or steam up the Potomac to throw shells into the Capitol was not within the range of possibilities. Yet all these things were prophesied, and descriptions of an iron monster, impervious to shot and shell, were so often repeated and told with such an air of knowing secrecy that the Merrimac became to the authorities at Washington a strange, foreboding spirit of evil, an intangible shape that would not be banished and that could not be struck —the Satan of the Civil War.

The Merrimac had been building for nearly a half year when Ericsson began the construction of the Monitor. But Ericsson's plans were more or less familiar and his engine freely discussed. It was known to be little larger than a pleasure steamer; and what could such a toy vessel do against the dragon of the South whose shape and powers had been multiplied by mysterious rumors and whispered warnings until even the lightest mention sent terror to the Federal heart?

"Mammie," said Virginia to the small, compact, gray-headed negro woman who came slowly along the gallery from behind the base of a tower, "Mammie, do you know which ship out there in the Roads is the Minnesota?"

"Don' know nuffin' 'bout de Yankee ships, Miss Virginia," replied the woman, placing a jar of roses upon a small bench in the shadow of the climbing vines, " 'ceptin' I hea Marse Harlan say las' evenin' dat de one ovah dar nearest de James is de Cumberlan'. Mus' be one o' de oders I reckon. What yo' want to know 'bout dat pa'ticula' ship fo', chile?" queried the black woman, pushing a stray lock of gray wool out of her eyes and looking quizzically at her mistress.

"The Minnesota is the ship to which Lieutenant Hamilton has been assigned, you know, Mammie."

" 'Tenant Hamilton! You mean Earl Hamilton, honey?"

"Yes, Mammie, you know he was in the United States navy and refused to go out with other Southerners at the beginning of the war. He has been stationed at Charleston, but I learned yesterday he had been sent to Hampton Roads and assigned to the Minnesota."

"Dat what yo' anxious 'bout dat pa'ticular ship foh, honey! Huh, huh," said the old negress, bending down to straighten up a budding rose, "I know jes' how you feel 'bout it, chile, I 'members when yo' an' Earl Hamilton an' Lafe Harlan played togeder in dis ole house day in an' day out—free of de purtiest children dat de sun evah shone fo', an' de happiest, too, I reckon." The old woman came and stood near Virginia, taking hold of her gown with a worshipful touch.

"I'm sure we were, Mammie. But the war has driven us in so many different directions I can hardly realize that this is Waverley or that we are the same beings you loved and chided in those dear old days."

" 'Deed it ain't, honey, an' deed yo' ain't. Wif Marse Eggleston off dar in Richmond tellin' Gen'l Lee how ter plan fo' ter feed de soldiers, Lafe Harlan in hidin' foh bein' a spy an I don' know what mo', an' yo' all heah alone wid de cares o' dis plantation on yo' purty shoulders, an' a lot o' lazy goodfo'-nuthin' niggahs worrying yo' life out—'tain't the same nohow. An' you say Earl Hamilton out dar on dat Yankee ship? Huh! One of dese nights dis yeah Yerrimac gwine out f'om Norfolk, an' open its big mouf, wiv its white teef longer'n my arm an' biggah'n de gate post yonner, and bite de Yankee ships in two in de middle, and swallo' ev'ry man on de decks, an' under de decks, an' dem dat has climbed in de riggin,' an' dem dat has jumped in de watah ter save deyse'ves—jes gwine ter roll its big eyes o' fiah an' open its monst'ous jaws an' swallo' 'em one after anudder jes as fast!"

"Hush, Mammie," cried Virginia, the color leaving her cheeks in spite of an attempt to laugh at the impossible creature the superstitions of the negress had conjured up. "That is a fate too cruel to wish even our Yankee enemies."

"Dat's jes what's gwine ter happen, honey. Eve'ybody say so, and moughty soon too," continued Black Mammie, nodding her head slowly in the direction of the ships. "I hear Cap'n Harlan talking to Squire Henderson las' night when dey drinkin' min' julep an' smokin' in the lib'ary. An dat's what he say gwine ter come ter pass, shuah."

"I hope it won't be so bad as that, Mammie, although I should rejoice to see the Yankees driven from this part of the country."

"Does that prohibition extend to me, Virginia?" cried a tall, well-formed woman, dressed in half mourning, coming from the house. "If it does, I'll go and begin packing at once."

"You are not the kind of Yankee I refer to, Cora, even though your home be in New Jersey, and the field of your triumphs Washington."

"No, I suppose not," replied the widow with a musical laugh. "Happening to have been your father's ward, and having been frequently brought by him into the heart of rebeldom before I was old enough to have any very clear ideas concerning the affairs of state, you think I have absorbed enough of your doctrines to be neutral. Well, your judgment may be right in my case, but I fear it will go wrong when it comes to Earl Hamilton. My opportunities for studying men have been better than yours, Virginia. The late Senator Poynter was not only a good husband but a helpful teacher; he taught me how to distinguish the genuine from the false article. And from what I know of Earl Hamilton he is a man of pronounced convictions. He proved it by refusing to follow the other naval officers in their resignations when the Sunny South rebelled. My, what a speech I am making, and on a warm morning, too. Mammie, hand me a chair and a fan."

Mrs. Poynter, having settled herself comfortably and opened the fan, began again to chaff Virginia, who still stood gazing in the direction of the ships.

"My dear, do you see putting off from the fleet a boat, in which is Lieutenant Earl Hamilton, of his majesty 'Marse Lincoln's' ship, the Minnesota," cried the older woman. "Is he coming to reply in person to a communication sent him by the conscienceless rebel, Virginia Eggleston of Waverley plantation? Because if you do," she went on, "it is time you were putting your tresses into the hands of Estelle, so that you may be made presentable. Love isn't so blind as he is painted, my dear, and the way to a man's heart is through the bowers of beauty."

"Cora, I believe you would jest in the presence of President Davis himself," said Virginia, throwing a swift glance in Mrs. Poynter's direction, and then turning again to the sea.

"Jest in the presence of President Davis! The saints forbid. Why, Virginia, if I am ever so fortunate as to come under the shadow of this idol of the Confederacy, I shall put my forehead in the dust at his feet and cry out—no, no, I shan't cry out, because if I did I should get my mouth full of earth, and I wouldn't do that for the greatest man that ever lived—not even Napoleon. But really, do you expect Lieutenant Hamilton to come here today?"

"You are curious," returned Virginia, nervously pulling a leaf from the vine above her head. "If I were versed in the arts and expressions familiar to those who have mingled in the society of the capital, perhaps I might be sure of a personal reply to my invitation. Being only an unsophisticated Virginia girl whose greatest accomplishments are to ride a horse, shoot a pistol, and know tobacco leaf from a yard of butternut, I shall probably fail."

"Virginia, my dear, you are getting on famously," cried Mrs. Poynter, applauding with her fan; "irony is becoming in you—it certainly is. When these bloodthirsty men get tired of killing each other and have time once more to think of entertaining a woman, I'll bring you out in Washington and create a sensation. I suppose you sent the letter you were writing this morning at an hour when any human being not distracted with love, or altogether insane, would have been too sound asleep even to dream."

"Yes, Cora, I sent it by Seth, and here he comes. We shall hear how he succeeded."

An aged negro, dressed in a broadcloth suit that had evidently been the property of his master, his snow-white locks puffing out in a great heap at the back of his head, his face shaded by a broad-brimmed manila hat, a yellow neckerchief tied neatly about his throat, came through the gate in the stone wall that surrounded the grounds, and along the winding foot path that led up to the house. Virginia ran down the steps to meet him. When she approached him, Seth took off his somewhat worn and broken manila covering, and stood with it in his hand.

"The letter, Seth. What did you do with it?" she inquired with poorly veiled anxiety.

"I couldn' gib it 'zactly ter Marse Hamilton, Miss Virginia. Dey say I cayn't come 'bo'd de ship 'count o' o'dahs, but dey took de lettah up ter de deck an' say dey'd delibbah it when he come back."

"Then he was not on the ship?"

"Not jes at de time I was dah, Miss Virginia. A man in a blue cap say he done gone ovah ter de fo't but'll be back 'bout ten o'clock. So I lef' de lettah an' come away like you tol' me."

"Very well, Seth. Go to the cellar, get a bottle of wine, and take it to Sis Tab at the quarters," said Virginia, turning back toward the house. Then after a moment's hesitation she continued, "Stop at the stables as you go and inquire after Bay Nellie. She strained her shoulder taking a ditch yesterday."

"Yas, Miss Virginia," replied the negro, with a respectful bob of his snow-white head.

"Then, when you return, you may put my pistols in order—the brace father brought to me from London. I may want to do some target practice."

The old family servant went away on his errands, repeating to himself the virtues of his mistress, who never neglected the poorest slave on the plantation in sickness or trouble. Virginia returned to the gallery, where she told Mrs. Poynter of Seth's failure to deliver the letter to Hamilton in person, but that he was sure to receive it early in the day, and, should he respond to her invitation, might be looked for at almost any time.

Mrs. Poynter listened patiently until Virginia had concluded, when she said with mock seriousness:

"Virginia, I am convinced you are the most shameless coquette alive. You know Hamilton loves you to distraction, and but for your father's pledge to the late Judge Harlan that you should marry his son, Lafe, you would have accepted the Lieutenant long ago. So far as your choice of Hamilton goes, I agree with you, but Captain Harlan is here now, risking his neck to speak to you."

"Am I to be blamed for that?" interrupted Virginia. "Must I drive from the house a man related to the family—the son of my father's life-long friend? I have told him over and over again that I cannot love him in that way; I can do no more."

"Yes you can, or rather you have."

"In what way?"

"Why, Miss Innocence, you have invited Lieutenant Hamilton, Harlan's dearest rival, to come here and visit you. Now, if they should meet, Virginia!"

"What do you mean?" exclaimed Virginia with sudden apprehension.

"Oh. nothing more than if they should meet, they will probably settle their differences in true chivalric style," said Mrs. Poynter, rising and striking the attitude of a fencer preparing for encounter.

"Surely it will not come to that." Virginia was pacing up and down the gallery in great agitation. "They were schoolmates in youth; can the war have so changed their relations?"

"Not the war, Virginia. When two men love the same woman, and she keeps them both in doubt, they are not likely to read poetry in concert."

"Mrs. Poynter," said Virginia, stopping suddenly in her walk and speaking with great earnestness. "There is, as you say, danger of a serious quarrel should Hamilton and Harlan meet in this house. I feel that. But what I have done I would not undo if I could. I have every reason to believe that the Merrimac, built over there in Norfolk, the ship which all the South believes to be impregnable, is preparing to attack the ships in Hampton Roads. I couldn't rest without warning Earl, who is dear to me through a thousand associations, of the awful fate that awaits him if he remains on board the Minnesota. Besides, he is a Southerner, born and bred. He has no right there."

"You are wrong, Virginia, very wrong," said Mrs. Poynter, rising and joining her foster sister. "There, dear, don't dispute me. If Lieutenant Hamilton were here, I might agree with you, because it never pays to admit to a man that any woman was ever wrong; but between ourselves, you are making a mistake. Lieutenant Hamilton is a man, and—men are scarce—at least men of Earl's type. Now that you have invited him to come here on a few hours' absence that he can beg, borrow or steal, I fear you are going to mar the time with arguments concerning the rights of a sovereign state and all the rest of it. Tell me and tell me frankly what reception you will accord Lieutenant Hamilton when he comes? You hesitate. Answer, I command you!"

While Mrs. Poynter had been speaking, Virginia resumed her restless walk up and down the gallery, her mind disturbed by many conflicting emotions. In her heart she knew she loved Earl Hamilton above all else in the world. Uppermost in her mind was the desire to see him and to warn him of his danger. And yet she tried to convince herself that her letter was inspired by a desire to bring Hamilton to Waverley, where, if at any place, he might be persuaded to abandon the Union and cast his lot with the South. Her patriotism was great, her belief in the right of the Southern states to secede from the Union unshaken. She knew, too, that Hamilton's patriotism for the cause he had chosen was no less than hers, and that neither the eloquent pleadings of his brother officers nor the scorn of her own words had caused him to waver from the course he had taken. While he was in Charleston and no immediate danger threatened him, she had led herself to believe that her faith in him was dead—that love for her country had crowded him out of her heart. But when she learned he had been ordered to Hampton Roads, and that he was to be stationed on board one of the ships marked for sure destruction by the Merrimac, all the old love flamed up in her heart with tenfold more power than before, and she resolved to sacrifice pride and womanly delicacy in an attempt to save him. When she wrote the letter inviting him to Waverley she had no well-defined plan as to her course, should he accept. All had been hazy, indistinct. Something she would do to keep him with her till the danger was past. Further than that she had no definite plan. And now, when Mrs. Poynter asked her to tell directly what she intended doing upon his arrival, she found herself unable to answer.

"Come to my room, Cora," she said at last. "I will try to tell you there."

A moment later the gallery was deserted. The sunbeams crept in and out of the vine-shadowed nooks and crannies of the rambling old house. A robin sang in a wide-spreading elm down by the big gate, and from the distant quarters stole the words of a negro lullaby:

> Bye-bye, ma' honey, twel de happy mawin';
> Bye-bye, ma' pickaninny chile.
> Bye-bye, ma' honey, twel de blessed dawin';
> Mammie comin' ter yo' arter while.

CHAPTER II.

WATERLOO WILLIS.

Seth sat in a shaded corner of the gallery, the name given to the veranda which extended around three sides of the house. Along the walls themselves the gallery was wide and roomy, but it narrowed to the width of a few feet where it ran around the bases of the great corner towers. There were four of these, built solidly into the walls, rising several feet above the roof, and giving to the house something the appearance of a castle.

From his sheltered perch in the niche formed by one of the recesses on the southeast front of the building Seth commanded a view of Hampton Roads, Newport News, Hampton, and Fort Monroe. Far across the Roads and straight on up the Elizabeth River, of which the mouth was just visible, were the Gosport Navy Yards, near Norfolk. In the channel, a few hundred yards from the north shore, lay the Union fleet, stretched out in a six-mile line from Newport News to the fort. The sails of all the ships were furled, and the small volumes of smoke, creeping lazily from the smokestacks and drifting away on the still air, gave evidence of a feeling of security in the minds of commanders and crews.

"What fo' yo' settin' out dar starin' at nuffin' like er owl in de noontime?" said black Mammie, halting in the doorway with her hands full of fresh mint. "Didn' I heah Miss Virginia tell ye ter put her pistols in o'dah? Youse gettin' mighty 'digenous in yo' ol' age. 'Specs putty soon we haf ter call yo' 'Marse,' same's ef yo' was white an' free, which yo' ain't, nudder de one nur de udder, nur gwine ter be nudder. Huh, better go on 'bout yo' work and stop yo' nonsense, *Marse* Seth! Golly, but dat do soun' scrumptuous!" and Mammie chuckled so hard she scattered sprigs of the pungent herb all about her.

Seth, piqued by her good-natured sarcasm, took one of the ivory-mounted pistols from its case at his feet, drew a piece of chamois skin from his pocket, and began to polish the barrel in rather a desultory way.

"What fo' yo' go on dat-a-way, Mammie? Don' yo' see I'se doin' my endeavorest. An' who done tole yo' I'se like ter be free?" The old negro paused in his labor to squint through the sights of the weapon.

"Huh! Nobody don' need tell me what I done knows myse'f, yo' ole brack fool. Ain' all de lazy niggahs in Virginia thinkin' 'bout gettin' dah freedom an' gwine way off up No'f somewha' an' bein' rich and 'spectable an' hev'en white folks call em Marse, an' all such foolsomenesses? Mammie hain' live all dese yeahs, a 'spectable membah ob dis ole Virginia fambly, 'thout knowin' what's gwine on roun' heah, deed she ain't. I done knows de niggahs bettah dan de Lo'd what made em, an' dey's all good fo' nuthin' loafums, dat dey is, an' no mo' fittin' fo' ter be free dan I is, huh!"

"Yo' been lis'nen ter Estelle talkin', dat who yo' been lis'nen ter, Mammie," replied Seth. "She all time say dis wa's gwine free de niggah. What he gwine do when he free, dat's wat I like ter know?" and Seth rested from his labor and looked inquiringly into the face of his companion. "When I wuz up No'f wi' ole Marse Eggleston," he continued, "I done seed niggahs an' white men, too—wu'kin' mighty sight ha'dah den niggahs ha' ter wu'k on dis plantation. Ef a niggah's got ter wu'k when he free, whar's de use? Huh, whar dat Brack Mammie gone? She dun run away f'um de truf like et wuz a blacksnake, he, he."

While Seth was delivering this bit of wisdom, a man came from behind the base of one of the towers and stood an interested listener. The newcomer was rather above medium height, somewhat thin of body and long of leg. His face was smooth-shaven, and his bright, blue eyes, glancing quickly over the premises, seemed to fix everything on the instant in his mind. He was dressed in a well-worn suit of gray cashmere, supplemented by a pair of cavalry riding boots, a blue flannel shirt, and broad brimmed gray beaver hat. A black neckerchief tied at the throat in a loose sailor knot completed his attire.

"Philosophy doesn't seem to observe the color line, even in the South," he mused, as Seth concluded. Then addressing the negro he continued, "You are a philosopher born."

Seth, surprised at being so suddenly recalled from his speculations by a stranger, and only partially comprehending the remark, hastened to say:

"No, sah, I'se done born right heah at Waverley, an' hain' nevah sarved nobody but jes' Marse Eggleston an' Miss Virginia."

The stranger laughed quietly at Seth's blunder and said: "All right, let it go at that. If you are Miss Eggleston's servant, you will drop that pretty shooting iron and inform her that a friend of the family is waiting for an interview."

"Yas, sah, yas, sah," said the negro, nervously putting the pistols in the case. As he was shuffling along the gallery he glanced toward the gate, and, halting suddenly, said in a tone of relief, "Huh, ef dah don' come Marse Henderson, shuah."

"Henderson? Who's he?" demanded the stranger.

"A Southern gen'man, sah, an' moughty 'sturbed 'bout de 'fec' ob dis wa' on his prop'ty."

"A large property owner, I presume?" said the stranger, mounting the steps and leaning easily against the base of the tower where he would be invisible to a person coming up the path.

"Used ter be, sah, but he grow hosses an' run em in de races, an' I hear ole Marse Eggleston say he done lose heap o' money in New O'leans, in dem cotton specellatums. Mus' been de truf, fo' all de prop'ty he got lef' 's one little dumb niggah boy, Joe."

"And he's afraid this remnant of a fortune is to be taken from him by the war? I see!"

"Dat's jes' it, sah. Nebbah lets dat boy outen his sight, and allus sayin' he gwine ter horsewhip him, but he nebbah done tech him in dat way, kase he think mo' o' dat useless runt o' a niggah dan Miss

Virginia do o' her Bay Nellie, an' dey ain't nuffin' mo' sacrifyin' dan dat, sah."

While Seth was speaking, a slender little negro boy, perhaps ten years of age, came through the gate. Glancing backward, first over one shoulder and then the other, like a pet animal seeking assurance of his master, he trotted up the path toward the house. He was followed a moment later by a short, rather stout man, dressed in a bleached linen suit, patent leather shoes, and a broad-brimmed white hat. His hair was rather long and curled upward where it fell upon his rolling shirt collar, but when he removed his hat and mopped his brow with a red bandanna, drawn with a flourish from an inside pocket of his coat, the dome of his head rose bare and polished above the gray-brown locks that grew no higher than the level of his ears. He carried a gold-mounted, ebony cane, and in walking raised himself on his toes with the air of one who controlled large possessions and held an assured position in the world.

"Maw'nin' Seth," he said, stopping a short distance from the house and surveying the premises with an air of ownership. "Don' reckon the ladies are stirrin' yet?"

"Deed dey is," replied the negro, "Miss Virginia done been out heah on de gallery evah since befo' daybreak. Went up stairs, her an' Miss Poynter, sho't time ago, sah, an' I hain' done seed 'em since. I'll look fo' 'em, sah."

"Don't disturb the ladies; they may be at breakfast—hah! Come heah, Joe!" The Squire had caught a glimpse of the man on the gallery, and instantly his manner changed. The air of pompous security gave way to a mixture of anxiety, entreaty, challenge and demand. Keeping his eyes fixed on the stranger, he swept out his cane with the gesture of a blind man and called again, with more affection than command, "Come heah, Joe!"

"Squire Henderson, I believe," said the stranger, coming forward with an air of easy familiarity from the shadow of the tower. "Glad to see you. Have a seegar?" As he spoke, he plunged his hand into a side pocket of his coat and brought up a handful of Havanas.

"Yo' name, sah!" demanded the Squire with great dignity, ignoring the proffered peace offering.

"Waterloo Willis, of Washington," replied the Yankee, striking a match and coolly lighting a cigar. War correspondent of the Washington Intelligencer."

"Yo' wah, sah, is a damnable outrage, and a menace to the rights o' property guaranteed by the constitution, sah. Come heah, Joe."

The closing sentence was made not as a demand, but as a fitting close to his protest. Although the Squire did not realize it, except in a vague, shadowy way, this small, dumb, black creature represented the negro property of all the South, and his frequent requests to the darky to keep near him were, in some measure, the expression of the old masters' feeling toward their chattels. It gave one a glimpse of the animal affection which existed between the two races.

"Don't get excited," said the correspondent, lazily puffing smoke into the vines. "I assure you, Mr. Henderson—"

"Squire Henderson, if yo' please, sah!" interrupted the Southerner, drawing himself up to his full height.

"'Beg pardon, Squire. I'm new in these parts and have lots to learn. I was going to say that your property is in no danger from me. I come here with the most friendly intentions, I assure you."

"Friendship is a holy word, sah, as Sir Walter Scott has said, at least in the South, sah," said the Squire, suddenly relaxing. "Have you seen Miss Virginia?"

"Not yet. I only arrived a few moments ago,

and was just sending a request for an interview when you came up."

"Then, sah," said the Squire, offering his hand with a great show of cordiality, "I give you welcome to Waverley."

"Obliged to you," said Willis, once more diving into his pockets. "Have a seegar?"

"I nevah smoke befo' evenin'," said the Squire, "but I'll accept the tobacco in the spirit in which it is offered, sah, for I perceive that yo' are a gentleman, sah."

"You're a man of keen perceptions, that's clear, Squire," Willis drawled, shoving his hands into his trouser pockets. Then standing with his feet wide apart he noted the peculiar architecture of the house. "Quaint conceit, Squire," he observed. "A mediaeval structure in the youngest of nations; rare combination."

"The house was built by Judge Eggleston as a so't o' monument to Sir Walter Scott, his favorite author. Got the idea out of Ivanhoe, I believe, sah."

At this moment a voice in one of the interior rooms was heard singing those sweetly sad words of the Scotch poet:

> Ye banks an' braes o' bonnie Doon,
>   How can ye bloom sae fresh an' fair?
> How can ye sing, ye little birds,
>   An' I sae weary, fu' o' care?

"The spirit of Bobbie Burns seems to have taken possession of the monument to Sir Walter, Squire. By Jimtown, what a pretty girl!"

This expression of surprise, uttered in an undertone, was occasioned by the appearance of a girl of fifteen or sixteen years. She came tripping through the door and ran down the steps into the garden, before she was aware of the presence of anyone save herself. A small, dark creature, with clear, olive complexion and big black eyes, like those of an animal, deep and splendid, but waiting only a touch to blaze with anger or melt with affection. Her rather tightly curling hair was surmounted by a tiny red cap. She wore a simple gown of plain brown muslin, cut low in the neck, and displaying a pair of round, dimpled shoulders and short but shapely throat. As she reached the lower step leading to the gallery, she paused suddenly, seeing the stranger, and stood a moment irresolute.

"Is it tiger or fawn?" was Willis' mental question.

"Maw'nin' Estelle," said the Squire, with a certain tone of familiarity, never used in the South to women of pure American blood. "Yo' are musical as a mocking bird at midnight."

The girl stood for a moment, looking from one

to the other of the persons in the little group. Then, throwing a hasty glance into the shrubbery and down the narrow path that led toward the James River, she turned suddenly, ran up the steps, and, bending above one of the potted plants that stood in rows along the gallery, said, with a nervous trill in her voice:

"Who could help singing, with all these sunbeams laughing in the arms of the roses?"

"Poetry, by Jimtown," said Willis.

"The picture would be perfect, sah, as she has so eloquently painted it, were it not fo' yo' Yankee encroachments on the rights of property," proclaimed the Squire; then, after a moment's hesitation, he called, "Come heah, Joe."

"Property, Squire?" said Willis, jerking his head in the direction of Joe, who stood quietly near the Squire.

"Yes, sah, property, according to the constitution as fo'mulated by that distinguished Virginian, George Washington," declaimed the old Southerner with a pompous wave of the hand.

Willis laughed softly, and Estelle, coming down the steps, approached him timidly and said:

"Are yo' all a Yankee soldier, sah?"

"A soldier of the pen, not of the sword, Miss Estelle," replied Willis.

The girl flushed at being addressed in this fashion. Pretty and intelligent as she was, and free to go and come as any member of the household, yet the slightly flattened nostrils, the deep, dark eyes, wide and full, the low brow, and the quick waves in her black hair raised the barrier of caste and made her slave. For the first time in her life she had been addressed as "Miss," and the new dignity sent the blood to her brain and lighted a new fire in her eyes.

"It's tiger," was the correspondent's mental note.

"Estelle is Miss Virginia's—h'm, Miss Virginia's waiting maid, sah," said the Squire, endeavoring to correct, without offending the girl, the mistake Willis had made. "Mr. Willis is only a newspaper co'respondent, Estelle."

"Correct as type, Squire," drawled Willis. "Only a newspaper correspondent, who gathers facts for some dull plodder to compile into a big book and sign himself historian."

"And the prejudices of the co'respondent make histories very unreliable affairs, sah."

"The honest correspondent, Squire, looks impartially at all sides of all things, wars included."

"Fo' a newspaper co'respondent yo' position is admirable, sah," answered the Squire, turning to lay his hand on the head of his dumb slave, "but fo' a man whose property is in dangah of bein' confiscated it is untenable, sah, untenable."

Having delivered this sonorous sentence, he gave an oratorical flourish; and drawing a newspaper from his pocket, began to scan its pages. Estelle, who, at a little distance, had been talking to Seth, now came up, and addressing Willis, said:

"But you all are with the Yankee army!"

"With it, but not of it," replied the correspondent, somewhat at a loss just how to address her.

"And the real soldiers?" inquired the girl, with an air of anxiety.

"Oh, they're all about here. I passed a brigade patrol of Von Benzinger's command on my way up. They seem to be on the scent of something. Some poor devil of a spy, I suppose."

"Another encroachment on the rights of prope'ty," said the Squire, crushing the paper in his hand and glaring at Willis. "Whar's Joe?"

"Well, I reckon we all don' need to be afeared as long as yo' are heah to protect us, Squire," said Estelle, with an attempt at merriment. Her nervousness, however, had increased greatly when Willis mentioned the patrol. "What's yo' paper, Squire?"

"Richmond Whig. I got it ovah to Little Bethel this mo'nin'. According to the print heah, our soldiers are driving in the Yanks all along the line."

"Bettah go ovah to the shady side o' the gallery if yo' goin' to read, Squire; and take Mistah Willis along. There's fresh mint on the sidebo'd," she added, seeing the Squire linger.

Henderson folded the paper rather hastily after this remark, and turning to Willis, said:

"Mighty pleasant mixture, mint julep, an' one indigenous to the South, sah. Will you join me?"

"My prejudices, if I have any, do not extend to mint julep, especially after a dusty walk on a hot morning. And besides," he added, following the Squire up the steps, "a late Richmond paper may prove interesting."

As soon as the Squire and Willis were well within the house, Estelle ran across the lawn to the path that led through the woods toward the James, and called softly, "Lafe! Lafe!" Getting no response, she came back slowly across the lawn, peering into the shrubbery on every hand. Seth put away the pistols he had been cleaning, and with the case under his arm started around the house.

"What you doin' with Virginia's pistols," said Estelle, halting in front of him.

"Cleanin' 'em, 'cordin' to Miss Virginia's o'dahs," said Seth.

"What's she going to do with 'em?"

"Shoot 'em at a target, dat's what she say, but cayn't tell what may happin wid all dese Yankee so'dgers ridin' deah hosses ober de plantation."

"I don't see why men should go to wah," said Estelle with a perceptible shiver.

"Moughty cu'ious wo'ld, Estelle, moughty cu'ious," said the old negro, putting the pistol case on a garden bench and sweeping the air with both arms at once. "Men readin' de good Book, preachin' brudderly lub, an' all de time 'ventin' machines ter kill each odder wid. Good Book say, man mus' wu'k an' he mus'n' fight. Niggahs all de time tryin' ter get away f'um wu'k, an' white man killin' each odder f'um Washington ter Richmon'. Seems like dey got de good Book turn' bottom-side up, like a skeered possum in a tree top. Ef dis heah wa' don' stop mighty sudden somfin' gwine drap shuah."

Having unburdened his mind, Seth took up the pistols and continued on his way. When he was gone, Estelle threw herself into a garden seat and began in a low sweet tone to sing again, "Ye Banks an' Braes o' Bonnie Doon." Something in the melancholy words and music seemed to give expression to her own thoughts. All morning she had felt a presage of danger, and when she came into the yard it had been with the hope of finding Harlan and confiding to him her feelings. She knew he was in hiding, a Confederate guerilla captain, and the danger, whatever it was, seemed to threaten him. To her simple mind this dashing Southerner, with his free ways and devil-may-care manners, was little less than a god. She knew better than anyone could tell her the gulf that divided them, the dark shadow that shut her out from all worth while in life to her—the love and protection of a free man. She hated her own race, because they appeared willing to bear the yoke of serfdom. Equal companionship with white people of the better class was denied her. And so, to this wild, reckless man, who had complimented her beauty and sat with her in the shadows, she had readily given her heart. If the North should triumph in the war, they told her slavery would cease, and although she could not but feel a certain prejudice toward the men who were invading the country of which she was, in a way, a part, yet her blood thrilled at the sound of the bugle notes from the white tents over at Newport News, and the sound of drums in the camps of the Yankees stirred her soul to dreams she dared not name, but from which Captain Harlan was never absent.

"Aren't you getting the words of that song a little tangled, Estelle?" said a voice behind her.

"Oh, Cap'n Harlan, whar have you been? I've

searched everywhere for you," cried the girl, springing up and running to meet him.

"What's happened now?" demanded Harlan, ignoring the tender look in her eyes. "Are the Yanks
up to any new tricks?"

"There's a man in the house just over from the
Union lines who says he saw a lot of soldiers riding this way, and they seemed to be searching for
someone. I saw 'em myself from a window in the
tower before he told me, and was coming to tell
you about 'em, when I found him here, talking to
Squire Henderson. The stranger told us they were
a brigade patrol of Von Benzinger's command."

"Who's the stranger?" demanded Harlan, fierce-
ly.

"Only a newspaper correspondent. You needn't
be afeared o' him, I reckon."

"I ain't afeard o' any man," said the guerilla, giving his long, black hair a scornful toss, "but a patrol o' bluecoats is different. Whar's Virginia?"

"In the house with Mrs. Poynter," replied the
girl, her face darkening.

"I must see her. Run and tell her I'm going
away, and ask her to come to the sitting-room at
once."

"I won't," cried the girl, with a sudden lifting of
the shoulders and a saucy toss of the head.

"What's that?" said Harlan, facing her, his cruel lips drawing back from his white teeth and a dark line growing between his brows.

The girl struggled to keep hold of the bit of independence which at his command she had seized, but she felt it slipping away, and knew that in the end she must do his bidding. The pledge of Judge Eggleston to Harlan's father had never been a secret in the household, and Estelle knew the story by heart. She knew that Virginia respected her father's wishes, and would not openly rebel against them. She knew also that Virginia lived in hopes of bringing him to consent to cancel the contract when he was convinced that such a union would bring her nothing but unhappiness. Knowing this, and with the vision of freedom before her, Estelle clung to the little ray of hope born of her love. But struggle as she might, the power of Harlan over her was not to be denied.

"I'd do mos' anything fo' yo', Lafe," she said, with all the determination she could summon. "Haven't I proved it? But if you want to see Miss Virginia, yo' mus' go fo' her yo'self!"

"And be captured by the patrol because of your damned obstinacy. Very well."

"I'll go, Lafe, I'll go," cried the girl, seizing his arm in a tremor of terror. "But if you've tol' me the truth, if yo' care fo' me, why should yo' always be runnin' after Miss Virginia?"

"This is no time for talking nonsense, Estelle," said Harlan, roughly shaking himself free. "My life's in danger and I must see Virginia."

"Forgive me, Lafe. I'll find her right away and tell her what you say." The octoroon ran up the steps and into the house, pausing in the doorway to throw him a pleading look.

"I must get rid o' her somehow," muttered the guerrilla, when she had disappeared in the shadow. "A jealous woman is not to be trusted. If it were not for this cursed Hamilton"—he started, suddenly, and drew his hat over his eyes, as a man appeared in the doorway. "His friend! Willis!" he cried, starting back and laying his hand to his pistol.

"Correct as to both charges," said Willis, coming quickly into the garden and stopping close to Harlan. "Hamilton's friend—Willis of Washington. Your memory's good and you reason like a lawyer." With this, the correspondent puffed a huge cloud of smoke into the air, shoved his hands deep into his pockets, and with his feet wide apart stood looking Harlan square between the eyes.

"What do you want here?" demanded Harlan, doggedly.

"News," replied the correspondent, puffing steadily at his cigar, "and I've got it. Your friend, Squire Henderson, kindly loaned me his Richmond paper. I ran across a paragraph which said that the Confederate States of America would give a large reward for one Lafe Harlan, who is in the pay of the Yankees. Outside of Hamilton, I'm the only man that knows of your former treachery to the Union. You have successfully played false to both sides."

"Devil!" snarled Harlan, half drawing his pistol.

"Keep your ammunition. You may need it more, later on," said Willis. "What about this reward?"

"It's a lie," muttered Harlan, "a damned Yankee lie!"

"A Yankee lie, in a Richmond paper! Possible, but not probable."

"What use will you make of it?"

"Show it to Miss Eggleston," said Willis, blowing a cloud of smoke in Harlan's direction.

"I see your game," Harlan growled. "You want me to leave here so that your friend Hamilton—"

"Are you going?" said Willis, moving a step nearer.

"Yes. You hold the best hand while you keep that paper. You will use it against me to help Hamilton with Virginia."

"Not if you go away."

Standing in the doorway, looking straight at him, * * * was Estelle.

"For the present, I'll go. But I'll win against you both yet. When you meet Hamilton, give him my regards and tell him I'll watch for a chance to pay 'em in person."

Harlan disappeared through the stone archway that led to the stables. When he had gone, Willis knocked the ashes from his cigar, puffed a cloud of smoke into the air, and watched it slowly dissolve. "The scoundrel is not lacking in wit," he mused. "He guessed what use I'd make of the news. Well, Cap'n Harlan, unless I'm greatly mistaken in the temper of Miss Eggleston, you're done for in that quarter. She's a rebel to the last comma, but straight as sunshine. If you stay here, she shall know you have proved traitor to both sides."

Willis turned to re-enter the house. Standing in the doorway, looking straight at him out of her big, black eyes, was Estelle. And in her hand she held the Richmond paper.

CHAPTER III.

SURPRISES.

When Willis saw the paper, so important to his plans, in the hands of Estelle, he felt a thrill of apprehension new to him. But long service on a metropolitan newspaper had taught him that coolness and self-possession were a man's friends in a crisis, so he merely puffed a little harder at his cigar and moved leisurely toward the house. In mounting the steps, a sudden noise in the distance attracted his attention. He glanced over his shoulder. When he turned again to the house, Estelle had vanished.

"The little minx, what can she be up to?" soliloquized Willis. "Richmond papers are scarce. If she has reasons for keeping Harlan in Virginia's good graces, she may destroy this one. I was a dunce to lay it down. I wonder if she overheard the little colloquy I had with this picturesque bandit? If she did she must have a pretty fair conception of his character."

"Ah, sah, I missed yo'," said the Squire, appearing in the doorway. "Fo' a newspaper co'respondent yo' education, so far as mint juleps are concerned, sah, seems to have been neglected. Yo' left a large part of the delicious decoction in yo' glass, sah."

"Mr. Willis!" cried a merry voice from the hallway. "Do let me pass, Squire. I am sure it can be no other than my old Washington friend. Why to be sure it is," cried Mrs. Poynter, pushing by the Squire and extending her hand. "How do you do, Waterloo? Welcome to Waverley! Why didn't you send word you were coming? Dear me, it does my heart good to see somebody from Washington again. Squire, a chair for my friend. O, never mind your cigar. The smell of a fragrant Havana is incense to my nostrils, especially when a man from the capital's at one end of it. And such a dear old friend, too! There, make yourself comfortable in the shade and prepare to tell me all the gossip." She threw herself on a narrow bench by the window, holding by her two hands clasped over the edge of the seat, leaned gracefully back against the window frame, crossed her daintily slippered feet, shook back her mass of gold-bronze hair from her forehead, drew a long sigh of relief, and cried:

"Well, what in the world are you waiting for?

Don't you see I am dying to hear that musical drawl of yours?"

"If I were to tell you what is uppermost in my mind at this moment, Mrs. Poynter, I should say you make one of the most charming pictures, just as you are, that my eyes ever rested on."

"Delightful! The true Washington flavor. Did you hear that, Squire? Well, listen and learn. If you have an ambition to succeed with women, study the speech of a man from Washington."

"From the standpoint of a Southern gentleman, I should say that the speech of Mr. Willis was bold, if not positively rude, mar'm. In fact, an encroachment on the rights—"

"Of prope'ty. Yes, I know, Squire, whar's Joe?" mimicked Mrs. Poynter. "My dear Waterloo, you have no idea what a world of trouble this war has brought to the Squire here. What from regret that he's too old to enlist, and fear that the abolitionists will confiscate his one little negro, he does nothing but drink mint juleps and quote the constitution from morning to night."

"I met the Squire when I first came, half an hour ago," said Willis, with a great show of earnestness, "and found him a most agreeable gentleman, Mrs. Poynter. I will not hear him slandered even by you."

"Your words do you credit, sah; I'm proud to meet a man from the No'th who appreciates a gentleman who, although debarred by circumstances from winning glory on the field of battle in defense of the constitution, is ever ready to sacrifice his life on the altar of female loveliness." Having uttered these words in a most grandiloquent manner, the Squire bowed deeply to Mrs. Poynter, and then, resuming his place in the doorway, felt awkwardly about with his cane, and cried, "Whar's Joe?"

"Your sentiments do you honor, Squire," said Willis, unsmilingly.

"That's the first real compliment the Squire has paid me this morning," said Mrs. Poynter, "and proves the influence of good example."

"Are you a guest at Waverley, Mrs. Poynter?" inquired Willis, lighting a fresh cigar.

"Yes, of my foster sister, Virginia. I've been here for a month."

"And I neither knew nor guessed it," said Willis, with an added drawl.

"I was of the opinion, sah, that a newspaper co'respondent either knew or guessed about everything," said the Squire, anxious not to be crowded from the conversation.

"Waterloo, that's too bad, and I'm terribly disappointed," cried the widow. "Here I've been flattering myself your visit was purely and solely to see me. If you didn't know I was here, why in the world did you come?"

"My original purpose was to see the mistress of this plantation, although I have not the honor of her acquaintance."

"I informed Miss Virginia that you wished to see her, sah, and she requested me to say she would see you very soon, sah," Henderson hastened to say.

"Find Virginia if you can, Squire, and tell her that Mr. Willis is a friend of mine whom I shall be proud to present."

The Squire went away to do Mrs. Poynter's bidding. When he was gone, Willis turned to Mrs. Poynter and said:

"My dear Mrs. Poynter, there are many reasons why no one in this house, or whoever may come here, should know of my real connection with the War Department. It was through the influence of the late Senator Poynter that I secured the confidence of Secretary Stanton and was given an appointment in the secret service. You were aware of the fact at the time, and I speak now so that you may not inadvertently refer to it, and thus, perhaps, spoil some pretty little plan I may have laid."

"You do just right, Waterloo. It might have

happened just as you say," said Mrs. Poynter, making an effort to be serious. "But now that you've warned me, I shall be on my guard. Only, if you do have any interesting secrets," she continued, in her usual gay manner, don't, for the life of you, hint of them to me, or I shall never sleep for wishing to know them."

"If you refer to professional secrets, my dear Mrs. Poynter," said Willis, "I can promise you obedience without reserve. But in return I must ask you not to request a confidence, for I shall find it hard to refuse you anything."

There was a thrill in his voice that brought a livelier color to Mrs. Poynter's checks, and she hastened to say:

"There now, Waterloo, you are going to be unnatural and I shall be forced to dislike you. Isn't this a beautiful old place?" she continued, in a half-embarrassed way.

"Very," drawled the correspondent, settling back in his chair and smoking furiously for a moment. "By the way, who is that interesting little Arab I met out here in the yard a while ago? A dark-skinned girl, all eyes and teeth. When I called her 'Miss' she came near fainting away, and the Squire went out of his way to correct me."

"You mean Estelle. I can imagine how the

Squire was shocked. She is the daughter of a favorite slave of Judge Eggleston's. Her mother died when Estelle was an infant. Virginia's black Mammie nursed her, and although she is a slave, she has always been allowed her liberty. She is supposed to be Virginia's hand-maid, but she does quite as she pleases, and is more or less spoiled. I can imagine how you shocked the Squire. The lines of caste are very closely drawn in the South."

"She's too pretty to be classed in the Squire's category of property. By Jimtown! I don't wonder Mrs. Stowe and Wendell Phillips and the rest of 'em are abolitionists!"

"Hush, here comes Virginia. Don't prejudice your introduction by such expressions."

"Mr. Willis," said the Squire, stepping briskly out upon the gallery, "allow me to present you to Miss Eggleston, who is, during the unavoidable absence of her father, the mistress of this plantation. Miss Virginia, Mr. Willis of Washington."

The Squire bowed low and swept the floor with his hat in an obsequious gesture.

"Welcome to Waverley, Mr. Willis," said Virginia, graciously extending her hand. "The Squire informed me you had a message for me. I hope you bring good news!"

"And I trust you will consider it so. I learned

this morning that a friend of mine, and, I believe, of yours, was in the neighborhood, and thinking war might keep the news from you, I made bold to come over from headquarters and tell you of it."

"A friend of mine? To whom do you refer?"

"Lieutenant Hamilton. He's been ordered to the Roads and is now stationed on the Minnesota."

"Earl Hamilton, on a Yankee frigate!" cried the Squire, his face flushing with anger. "He's a disgrace to the South, sah. A promisin' young Virginian ruined by the prejudices taught at Annapolis!"

"Don't use hard words, Squire, they don't become you," said Mrs. Poynter, tapping him lightly on the arm with her fan. "And oh, you great big stupid!" she continued, turning to Waterloo. "The news you bring is stale, flat, and unprofitable. We knew all about it yesterday, didn't we, Virginia?"

"O, yes," replied Virginia, the color mounting her cheeks. "Lieutenant Hamilton is an old friend of the family, and we were certain to know of his arrival. But it was very kind of you to think of us, Mr. Willis. Then you and Earl are old acquaintances?"

"Yes, I was detailed to look after the news of the fleet off Charleston, and we became fast friends."

While they were speaking, little Joe had plucked

a rose from one of the plants blooming on the gallery, and slipped it into the Squire's hand. The Squire brought it to the level of his nose, looked at it quizzically for a moment, and then, with a hint of moisture in his eyes, turned to the boy, and said:

"You little thieven' scoundrel! Ef I catch you a pullin' Miss Virginia's flowers, I'll rawhide yo' till yo' white." Then to Mrs. Poynter he made a sweeping bow and presented her with the rose.

"Your property, Squire, seems to be developing a soul," she said, with a light laugh. "I shall treasure this as a most eloquent and convincing argument against the 'rights o' prope'ty according to the constitution.'"

"Your sentiment, Mrs. Poynter," said the Squire, bowing again, "does honor to yo' heart, but violence to the constitution."

"You have a quaint old place here, Miss Eggleston," said Willis, when they had done laughing at the little scene in which Joe had unwittingly been the chief actor. "And quaint people as well. I found your old servant to be quite a philosopher in his way."

"We are little understood at the North," replied Virginia, gazing thoughtfully in the direction of the quarters. "The negroes are a race of philosophers. It is those who are striving to destroy their homes and poison their peaceful lives who lack philosophy. But—come, let's take a little stroll through the grounds. I've been up since daybreak, but the morning has been so filled with duties I have not had an opportunity to get a breath of the woods."

Together they went down the broad steps of the gallery and moved about under the trees along the winding paths until they came to the edge of the wood. Here Virginia turned back, while the other three continued along the path toward the James, Mrs. Poynter's merry laugh making a pleasant accompaniment to the murmur of the distant waters.

Virginia went slowly back toward the house, her mind full of conflicting emotions. What would Earl Hamilton think of her letter? When they parted, she had thought it was for the last time. There had been hasty words on both sides. She believed herself in the right then, and time had not changed her opinions. Had he remained at Charleston or been ordered anywhere else, it might have been different. But Harlan's assurance that the Merrimac was to attack the Union fleet very soon, perhaps today, had alarmed her. To save an old friend from certain death—this was her first duty. After that—

A sudden shout down the shell road beyond the stone wall was followed by the sharp crack of a pistol. There were shouts, orders, and the tramp of hurried feet. Estelle, running through the gate from the road, rushed past Virginia, who stood near the house. "Lafe!" panted the girl, as she flew up the steps to the gallery. When she reached the door nearest the gate, she stood a moment irresolute. Then she threw it wide open, turned quickly, drew herself to her full height, and with blazing eyes, clenched hands, and tightly drawn lips, stood like a bronze statue framed by the doorway, waiting.

CHAPTER IV.

A RESCUE.

Virginia was standing half way down to the gate, when Harlan darted past her into the house, closely pursued by three of the soldiers. As he plunged through the open door, one of his pursuers fired his pistol, and the bullet, plowing into the woodwork of the casement, threw out a splinter which struck and crimsoned the cheek of the fugitive. The other two men did not stop, but the instant Harlan was inside, the door was shut and solidly bolted by Estelle. The soldiers hurled themselves vainly against it. A dozen other soldiers quickly arrived, and, under the direction of a corporal, surrounded the house. Evidently Harlan had run upon a post of the brigade patrol, and the entire squad had given chase.

Virginia, pale and terrified for an instant at the sudden rush and the firing, now flushed angrily, and going straight to the corporal, fronted him squarely, and said, "What authority have you, sir, to attack the inhabitants of this house?"

"That's my business, ma'am," said the corporal, coolly, "I'm in command of this squad."

"I am in possession of this house, my friend, and it becomes decidedly my business, when you bring your shooting ruffians upon these premises. And let me tell you, sir, that your officers shall hear of this outrage."

In her heart she was mortally afraid it was all over with Harlan, but she had the strength to appear confident.

"I think your friend'll just about swing for a spy, that's what I think," said the non-com, with the air of concluding the interview. And with this reassuring opinion, he ordered three of his men to try all doors and windows. Another he sent for an axe to have in readiness to beat down the door.

The situation was desperate, for if Harlan were once captured, there would be no trouble in establishing his identity. And it was for her—through his blind, unreasoning love of her—that he was here, an inch from death.

The men who had been looking for an open door or window were not very anxious to find it. It was too easy to shoot through. So they reported everything firmly locked. The man with the axe returned. Four or five smashing blows near the bolt shattered the hasp, and the door was pushed open. At the same instant a pistol shot rang out in the rear of the house. A mounted officer, accompanied by his orderly, came trotting down the shell road, and perceiving the excitement, spurred through the gate and pulled up close to the veranda, the soldiers coming to attention and saluting.

"What's all this?" he asked.

As if in answer to his question, four troopers came around the house with drawn sabers, escorting Harlan, whose cheek was bleeding from the splinter. One of the troopers had a bullet through his hand.

"Who's this?" demanded the officer.

The corporal gave the saber salute and replied: "Sir, this man was fooling around our post. He didn't see us and he wouldn't halt when ordered. We chased him here."

"Who are you, then?" asked the officer, addressing Harlan.

"I'm a visitin' in this house, General von Benzinger, and your men have no right to arrest me."

"Visiting?" The General glanced at Virginia, started slightly, and took a good full look. Raising his hat, he swung off his horse, and said, politely,

"I have not the honor of knowing you, Mademoiselle, but are not you Miss Eggleston?" He spoke
with a slight, very agreeable accent, as of a French-
man who had lived in England.

"I am," replied the girl, "and if you are really
General von Benzinger, I protest against this unjustifiable arrest of my cousin, here in my house."

"Ah! Your cousin?" said the General, in a tone
of suave inquiry. "He is a non-combatant?"

"He is here visiting me—he is not here as a combatant."

The General raised his shoulders and eyebrows
the least bit. "And his name?"

"My name's Robertson," said Harlan, doggedly.

"But why do you not let the lady answer? Does
she not know the name of her cousin? What is
your cousin's name, Miss Eggleston?"

Virginia's face became crimson, as she answered,
"He has told you." The delicately veiled irony laid
by the General upon the words "your cousin" implied skepticism, and instead of being able to re-
sent it, she was forced, tacitly, at least, to lie to this
man who suspected her of lying. Beneath the boor-
ish stare of the soldiers and the coldly amused eyes
of the General, she was blushing furiously—angry
at her lack of self-control, terrified by the dreadful

consequences to Harlan if she should unwittingly reveal his identity.

"Withdraw your squad!" said the General, suddenly, and the soldiers jumped in obedience. Reaching the gate, with his men, the corporal halted them, uncertain whether their dismissal was final.

Virginia was grateful for the diversion, which enabled her to get control of herself. Von Benzinger did not conceal his admiration for the girl's face and its changing emotions.

"Miss Eggleston," he said, "I choose to believe you. This is your cousin, Robertson, a non-combatant. The soldiers have therefore no business to arrest him. He is free."

"Much obliged to ye," said Harlan, with a deep breath of relief.

"I do this upon your representations, Miss Eggleston," continued Von Benzinger, ignoring Harlan's existence. "But you had best urge your cousin to postpone his visit. May I have a private word with you?"

Harlan's face darkened at the cavalier dismissal, but he was hardly in a position to remonstrate, and he quickly disappeared through the battered doorway. The soldiers, seeing that their late prisoner was free, started down the road outside the wall.

"Corporal!" called Von Benzinger. "Under no

circumstances will you again molest the inhabitants of this house."

The corporal saluted and marched away, growling out a string of oaths under his breath, and consoling himself as best he could with the possession of Harlan's beautiful pistol.

The General dismissed his orderly, and after the man had ridden away, old Seth, timidly peering after the retreating soldiers, came out of his hiding place and closed the great iron gates. The General observed it, smiling. "I seem to be your prisoner now," he said. Virginia was about to call to Seth to open the gates, but the General waved his hand, stopping her.

"Let me be shut in with you a moment," he said. "It is long since I have talked with a refined girl. Do not deny me." He threw the double reins over the horse's neck and let the animal graze. "Let the gates shut out the war, and here in your garden let us be, not a Federal General and a Confederate girl, but simply a lady and a—gentleman."

"You will find me just a country girl, sir, but if you wish to stay, I am under such obligations to you—"

Oh, no, Mademoiselle—not that—if it is merely obligation, I will not force my society. I flattered myself you might be willing—"

"I am willing, General von Benzinger; I am very, very grateful for what you have done, but—well, truly, I cannot shut out the war—it touches me too nearly, too terribly. I should feel disloyal could I chat with you, forgetting you are an enemy."

"Have I then proved myself such an enemy?" he asked, looking at her intently.

"You know you have been very considerate, and —still you are fighting us—me, my brother, my father, my—my country."

"Miss Eggleston," said he, suddenly, "Is Lafe Harlan really your cousin?"

Virginia started and made a visible effort to conceal her alarm.

"I did not know," he went on. "I saved his life because I thought you wished it. I thought him more than a cousin to you, and when I saw you, beautiful in your distress, I saved him. I am not generous enough to do it silently—I wish you to know that I know all, and still, for your sake, I saved him."

Virginia, thrown into dire confusion by this revelation, was spared the embarrassment of a reply by a merry voice inside the house.

"Virginia, what have you been doing to this door? —I declare— What will you do next? Have you been using the house for a target—Oh, Lord!" Mrs. Poynter was tripping down the steps, and her last remark was occasioned by the sight of the Federal General.

"My sister, Mrs. Poynter—General von Benzinger."

"Goodness me, yes, of course—why, I saw the General at the President's reception last year—only then you were Monsieur von Benzinger—but I heard all about you. We couldn't understand the French title on the German name."

"I heard of, and, from a distance, admired Senator Poynter's wife, the wit of Washington. And how is the Senator?" inquired Von Benzinger, politely. "Is he well?"

A pained look shot into the face of the merry Cora. "He's dead," she said. Von Benzinger's features were a study. To make such a blunder cut him to the quick, and he stood speechless.

Mrs. Poynter, seeing his lugubrious and helpless face, lost the expression of pain, and suddenly burst out laughing. "I declare," she said, "if this had happened to anybody else I should scream."

"I beg a thousand pardons," he said, and bit his lip with vexation. "I have been engrossed—I had not heard, I—" he paused at a loss—the situation was hopeless.

"Do be considerate, Cora," said Virginia, "even if you don't mind seeming heartless."

Von Benzinger thanked her with his eyes, and Mrs. Poynter regained her composure.

"It was shocking of me to laugh—I, I beg your pardon." She smiled sweetly at Von Benzinger, who was never more thoroughly uncomfortable in his life. He prided himself upon not being a fool, and was habitually master of the situation.

"You are in a new role, are you not, with your shoulder straps?" asked Mrs. Poynter, saying the first thing to make conversation. "You were a ship-builder, or naval constructor, or something, weren't you? All Washington was talking about your proposed ironclads."

"I served in the Crimea," he replied. "My friend, the Duc de Chartres, is on McClellan's staff, and he told his chief about me. Hence my shoulder straps. My plans were rejected by the President's naval officers. They will regret it." There was a fierce look in his eye for an instant, but his face softened as he turned to Virginia, and said, "I must be going, something may happen before long—before I return. By the way," he said, glancing at the house and down toward the sea, "my brigade has received orders to move further inland, and the soldiers will be all about your house here. The Confederates will move up close to this point today. But be assured, there will be no battle, and you shall not suffer from my men. Have I not proved that? Your cousin, however, might again be mistaken for a combatant, and I should advise him to go to the Confederate lines before my troops arrive."

"I will tell him what you say," answered Virginia. "I am very grateful." She gave him her hand.

"Dear me! what has happened?" exclaimed Mrs. Poynter. "I've been out in the woods. Were the soldiers here?" Mrs. Poynter caught the warning look on Virginia's face and checked herself.

"I'll tell you all about it, dear—later. The General has been very good to us."

"Here, Thetis," he called. The trim black mare —three of her feet being white, she was named for Homer's sea-nymph, the silver-footed Thetis— looking up from the grass, tossed her shapely head, trotted up and put her soft nose in her master's hand. Von Benzinger swung himself lightly into the saddle. His fatigue blouse fitted perfectly his deep chest and small waist. He lifted his broad-brimmed black compaign hat, showing his snow-white, wavy hair which made a startling and effective contrast with his black Van Dyke beard. "Good morning, ladies," he said. "I hope I shall see much of you." Whirling his horse he started briskly down the driveway, having forgotten the closed gates. Seeing them, he reined in.

"Oh, the gates!" said Virginia. "Wait, General, I'll call Seth."

"Would you keep a General waiting for a servant?" said Mrs. Poynter, banteringly. "No, I'll just have to be his orderly and trot down there myself." Mrs. Poynter was secretly glad of the opportunity to see a little more of this polished General. "You forgetful genius," she said, changing from mock resignation to mock reproach, "why didn't you lead your horse down there and save us this trouble?"

"Not for the world would I trouble you, Mrs. Poynter," said the General. He measured with his eye the four and a half foot wall and the six-inch iron spikes atop of it. Then he bent forward and gave spur, and the black mare shot at the wall. It looked suicidal—as well ride at a house. There was a sudden gathering and unfolding of power—a leap —the black mare lengthened and rose in the air, cleared the spikes by an inch, and descending, caught her balance. Von Benzinger, turning back in the saddle, swept his hat far back in a graceful bow and rode away.

CHAPTER V.

VON BENZINGER.

General Hugo von Benzinger rode down from Waverley to the bay that peaceful, perfumed morning of the early spring. He drank in the glory of green leaves, the scent of flowers among the grass, and the notes of hidden birds; his heart grew tender with beauty and he dreamed. Virginia haunted him. Her face, with its slightly aquiline nose and clean-cut lips, was so firm and yet so childlike. He tried to remember the exact shades in her lustrous eyes; he could see plainly the long lashes, and the point of fine black hair breaking the oval of the straight forehead. He saw again the health of her fair complexion, browned a little by the sun, the rose-tinted cheek, the supple strength of her figure; and more than all, he heard still her slow, sweet, southern voice—a contralto speaking voice—

like the deepest flute notes he thought—a virginal
voice—and happy the man who should awaken in
it love's warmer tones.

As he had told her, it was long since he had
talked with a fine woman. He had dealt roughly
with rough men; and his life had been one battle.
Now, as he rode to the bay, his mind ran back in
flashes over that chequered life—the first memories
of his childhood in Spain, and the Madonna-like
peasant of Cadiz, who was his mother—her death
and his Strasbourg boyhood in the courtly house of
his father—his father's death, and he a nameless out-
cast—now before the mast in the French navy; now
in the iron mills till he became foreman; now a
student of engineering in the Latin quarter; now a
soldier—sergeant at Alma, lieutenant at Inkerman,
captain at Balaclava, and colonel at Sevastopol; and,
at last, in 1858, a famous man—constructor of the
steam frigate "La Gloire," the first ironclad, whose
name—Glory—revealed the main motive of his life.
Then in Paris he was somebody, and remembering
the manners of his boyhood, he perfected the polish
which had just pleased Miss Eggleston and charmed
Mrs. Poynter.

But although "La Gloire" was the most talked-of
vessel in Europe, although Napoleon III ordered
two more vessels like her, although the British ad-

miralty felt constrained to construct the ironclad "Warrior" as an offset to the French ships, yet the world was indifferent, and the naval profession itself only half believed in Von Benzinger's revolutionary idea. Paris, of course, while accepting him for his success, amused itself at his expense. Von Benzinger was the only man then living who fully realized the tremendous superiority of iron over wood upon the sea.

When, therefore, civil war grew imminent in America, Von Benzinger hastened to this country, hoping to test in battle ships like his "La Gloire." Since the completion of the armored frigate he had evolved in his mind the idea of a still stronger vessel, of which the sides should be inclined so that shot would be deflected, and which should be provided with a beak for striking an antagonist below the water line. But in this country he lacked the necessary influence and the knowledge of how to pull the wires. He was still without a hearing when the young Duc de Chartres, the Conte de Paris, and the Prince de Joinville joined McClellan—the two former as his aides. The young noblemen called McClellan's attention to Von Benzinger's astonishing military record in the Crimea, and soon afterward the veteran colonel was offered a brigadier's commission. He accepted it, and by help of his new connections got a hearing for his plans. The President appointed a board of naval officers to investigate the subject of armor-plating, and Von Benzinger exulted in his prospective success. The board, however, proved unenthusiastic and even skeptical in regard to the entire subject of armor-plating; and to Von Benzinger's intense chagrin, it reported adversely upon his proposition to convert frigates of the Minnesota class into iron-clads. Shortly afterward, the disappointed naval constructor heard the Confederates had raised and docked the sunken Merrimac at Gosport Navy Yards, near Hampton Roads. To the amazement of the Duc de Chartres, who knew Von Benzinger's consuming thirst for military distinction, the newly appointed brigadier, for some unknown reason, asked for service, not with the fighting army of the Potomac, but with the garrison of the Department of Virginia, stationed at Fort Monroe. There he and his proposals were forgotten, and as far as Washington was concerned, the constructor of "La Gloire" dropped into obscurity.

Six months later, when the vague terror of the Merrimac began, like a dim eclipse, to darken the nation and shed disastrous twilight, the President uneasily appointed another board to investigate the armor-plating adopted by France and England. But

Von Benzinger, who knew more about that plating than any other man alive, scornfully refused to submit his plans a second time. "They had their chance; they lost it," was his grim comment.

John Ericsson, however, the inventor of the screw propellor and the caloric engine, laid before the board his plan for the construction of floating batteries almost wholly of iron. The board promptly rejected this wild scheme. Then the Swedish inventor, unlike his fiery rival, Von Benzinger, went patiently before the board, and in an hour's talk convinced the naval officers that his plan was practical and based on sound theory. Reversing their original decision, they recommended to Naval Secretary Welles the construction of a floating battery according to Ericsson's plans, and under his personal superintendence. The Secretary orally authorized Ericsson to go ahead.

These things—his successes and disappointments—the contrasting scenes of his life, passed before Von Benzinger's mind, as he rode through the quiet woods. The road emerged from a tract of thick scrub oak, descended a slope, crossed a small tidewater stream, and ascended the opposite bank. At this point began the sandy, treeless levels which ran down to the shore. Here Von Benzinger halted. Immediately before him was one of his regiments, breaking camp. The bugle was sounding "the general," the signal for striking tents, and at one and the same time every tent in the regiment swayed over and came flat to the ground. There was much bustling of blue-shirted men, and very quickly, where trim rows of canvas walls had stood, there were only lines of neat white bundles, ready to be loaded on the pack-mule train, now hurrying with the customary kicks and squeals out of the brigade corral. The regiment was going back on the picket line, about a mile from Camp Butler and very close to Waverley. Reports had come to General Wool that Mugruder was coming too close.

"They do things better than they did at Bull Run," was the General's approving comment upon their manner of breaking camp. He did not, however, seem much interested in the proceedings of the regiment. His eyes passed over the swarming camp ground, over the black line of the Newport News batteries, where the artillerymen were lounging in the shade of the big guns, over the sunlit wash of waves to the Union warships anchored in the Roads. Boats full of sailors, on shore leave, were putting off toward Hampton town. Other boats were returning almost empty, barges and cutters and "bum-boats" were at the booms, the rigging was strung with drying clothes. From the looks of the fleet you would have said the country was at peace.

"Good!" exclaimed Von Benzinger, "They do not believe in ironclads. We shall see." He took his field glasses from the saddle, and through them looked across the Roads, scanning the line of the Elizabeth River. In the blue air, above the point of woods between the river and the Roads, hung a cloud of coal smoke no bigger than a man's hand.

"The Merrimac has finished coaling," murmured General von Benzinger, "she is getting up steam. Before night falls, Mr. Gideon Welles will believe in ironclad ships."

"Yes," he mused, "and so will Virginia Eggleston, the fair Confederate."

The sun was shining upon Hampton Roads. Far to the northward, off the Atlantic coast, a storm was raging. Her low deck swept by the heavy seas, cascades of water pouring under her turret and drenching the submarine berth-deck, on her way from New York to Washington, sank and rose the Monitor, plowing through that storm.

CHAPTER VI.

HAMILTON.

Returning to the Minnesota from his official visit to the fort, Lieutenant Earl Hamilton ran lightly up the steps from the cutter to the quarter deck. He was a splendid fellow—over six feet—a two hundred pounder in perfect condition—with huge chest and long, powerful arms—a clean-cut, gray-eyed, square-jawed, American sailorman—simple, healthy, and strong, in body and soul.

Going to the junior officers' cabin, he found awaiting him the note, sealed with the Eggleston crest and addressed in Virginia's well-known hand —to him. Odd that such a big animal's heart will thump twice as fast at the sight of a bit of daintily scratched paper! The Lieutenant sought solitude and sat down, carrying the note as though it were a great, gauzy butterfly, from the wings of which must be brushed no golden dust. Cutting the paper close about the seal, he unfolded the sheet and read:

My Dear Earl:—

I am very cross at you. Here you have been literally within sight of us for nearly a week—

"Yes, two days," commented Earl.

—and we have had no word or glimpse of you.

"Blessed inconsistency!" exclaimed Earl. "The last time I saw her she said, 'never let me see you while you wear that hated uniform.'"

Of course, I was terribly hurt and angry when you first told me you meant to desert the South, and I may have said more than I meant. But I do want to see you, Earl, very badly—and there is a serious reason why it must be today. I cannot tell you this reason until you come. You must come, and I will accept no excuse about not being able to get leave. You must come.

Your obedient servant,
VIRGINIA EGGLESTON.

WAVERLEY, March 8, 1862.

Fifteen minutes later, a big naval lieutenant was ashore, in the street of a light artillery battery, brazenly borrowing the horse of an astonished subaltern, whom he had never in his life seen before.

"Thanks, old fellow," he called to the owner, as he mounted, "I'm only going a mile, and I won't hurt him." The Lieutenant rode well for a sailor, and went dashing past regiment after regiment till he breasted the barren rise, crossed the stream, and struck into the scrub-oak woods through which Von Benzinger had ridden down but a short time before. Today these two men were ignorant of each other's existence, tomorrow they would be mortal enemies, face to face in their death struggle. Had Von Benzinger seen the naval officer riding that morning toward Waverley, many a wild scene of that Saturday night and Sunday morning would never have been acted. Upon a circumstance so slight depended the fates of these men and this woman. Unconscious of the dread control of things to come, Hamilton cantered briskly through the woods. Like Von Benzinger, it was long since Hamilton had talked with a fine girl. It wouldn't have mattered, however, if he had talked with one, unless she happened to be this particular fine girl, Virginia, who, for years, had absorbed all his great capacity for loving. His love for her was the undercurrent of all his thinking and living. He couldn't get away from it. It was there, tugging at him day and night, near her or far from her. Naturally, his love had made him very unhappy, since the war first rent the nation, and, as it then looked, had torn her from him. No Southerner who remained true to the old flag had sacrificed more for it than he, for he had given up his hope of winning her—his very heart. Perhaps only a man who has learned obedience as a sailor learns it—a man who knows how to submit his own desires to a higher law—is capable of such love as Hamilton felt for Virginia. Now, when he was actually coming back to her, as in the old days, love rose from the depths of his heart and seemed to fill his lungs deeper and deeper, and spread through his brain, and throbbed in all his blood, and took possession of his will. He turned down the shell road and saw the ivy-grown, familiar walls of Waverley, and the places his memory had consecrated to her. And off there, under the trees, the great magnolia blossoms swaying, indolent, behind her, was she herself—alone—waiting for him. He dismounted and threw the bridle rein over a spike on the wall. She was facing the bay, his back was toward it as he came up to her.

"How are you, Earl?" she said.

"I'm happy, Virginia—happier than I ever thought I'd be again." He looked as if he was dying to kiss her, but didn't dare. "And you, dear girl?—I declare, you look happy yourself."

"I'm not, though, Earl. No, I'm most unhappy, and that is why I sent for you. Why did you make me write, you naughty boy."

"How could I come, dear one? After what you said last spring, how could I come?"

"Last spring? And in a whole year mayn't I change my mind? You great—*man.*"

He heard the playful tenderness of her voice, he saw the happy curving of her lips, the glad dwelling of her eyes on his, and rapture seized him. Impulsively he tried to catch her in his arms. She pushed him back with her hand.

"Wait!" she said, and then realization of the implied promise in the word crimsoned her face. "Oh, I didn't mean that," she cried. "You mustn't, indeed you must not, Earl."

"You madden me, Virginia. You hold your love before me, so close, so dear, and then—"

"Then? Why, then, I ask some proof of *your* love, Earl."

"My love?" he cried. "Virginia, from that Christmas day, four years ago, when I came back to Waverley and found the little girl a woman—a child-woman, if you will—you know that I have loved you. I didn't know a man could love a woman so! And it's been mostly hopeless love, Virginia-girl. I knew your father wanted Lafe to have you; but—I couldn't help believing you cared more for me. That made it worse, dear one, to feel I was so close to winning you, and yet I could not. And when, last year, you refused me, sent me away, called me a traitor, I would have welcomed death in battle; yes, I cursed my life, I cursed my state, I cursed the South, whose insane rebellion took you from me."

"Yes," she said, bitterly, "you cursed the South, your own land, your own people. Why, Earl, you cursed *me* when you cursed the South."

"Oh Virginia, do not begin that again. It tears my heart—I cannot stand it."

Virginia, standing so that her eyes could catch the frigate Congress, suddenly noticed a great change in the looks of the ship. Men were swarming over the yards, the drying clothes were stripped from the rigging, the furled sails were flapping open, boats were swinging up on the davits, and the decks were alive with hurrying men. Steaming out of the Elizabeth River, could she have seen it, was the strange shape of the Merrimac, in full view now of the Union fleet. But Virginia did not need to see, she felt, she knew. "The Merrimac!" she thought, and, turning pale, she gave a little gasp of fear. Earl's own emotion kept him from seeing the cause of hers, and in an instant she had mastered herself.

"You are right, Earl, we cannot talk of that," said she. He must not see the ships, she must keep him

"Come," she said, giving him her hand, and turning away from the bay.

out of that hopeless battle. "Come," she said, giving him her hand, and turning away from the bay. "Come, say 'how do you do' to the dear old stump where the teeter-board was."

"The teeter-board?" he said, turning with relief from the gulf that neither he nor she could cross, and delightedly walking hand in hand with her. "Do you remember the teeter-board? Dear me, it seems like yesterday—or, rather—when you think of all that has come since, and how impossible it is to bring back that sweet old time—why, then, it seems like a dead life in some other world."

"Yet, we are the same two people," said she.

"The very same," he answered, "and if you loved me, Virginia, we would be the same forever."

"If you loved me," she said, "you would do something for me."

"And what may that something be?" he asked.

"Oh, say you'll do it."

"And then, perhaps, I couldn't. I must know."

"Stay here with me today."

"Now, queerly enough, little girl, that is precisely what I mean to do."

"You don't have to go back to the ship at all today?"

"Not at all, today. I've leave till morning. The Captain grumbled, but I got it."

"Then promise me you won't go back today."

"Why promise, sweet? I do not mean to go."

"But promise, promise me you'll stay."

"It's very sweet, little one, to have you so earnest about it."

"Then promise.".

"Well, I promise."

"You won't go even if the Merrimac attacks the fleet."

"You needn't worry about that, I guess."

"But, if it does?"

"Is the Merrimac your serious reason why I should come here today?"

She did not answer.

"The Merrimac has been a bugaboo too long," he said. "We do not think of her. But if you thought my ship today would be in battle, would you have me here—a coward?"

"No coward, Earl, no man can call you that. But the Northern sailors have no hope—their vessels will be crushed, and you—what right have you—a Southerner—to share their fate? You have no business there."

"You know I have, Virginia." His voice was very quiet, very firm.

From the bay came the sound of a big gun. They stood an instant, listening. Then came the roar of many.

"That's no salute," he cried with alarm. "The Merrimac has come."

Quickly he made a step to go, and was detained by Virginia's arms. "Earl! Earl!" she said, "I love you, Earl."

For an instant he forgot the booming guns, his ship, his duty—everything in the whole world, but the clasp of her arms, the light in her eyes, and the blending of her soul with his. Their lips met, and in that kiss their stubborn wills forgot their struggle and were one.

The thunder of the guns burst forth afresh.

"My ship, my ship," he groaned, struggling in his heart to break the toil of love. "I must go— quickly—now."

He had to use force to free himself. "Oh, you do not love me, you do not care for my love," she moaned.

"I swear, Virginia, by all holy things, I love you better than life, than everything, than all the world."

"Prove it, then. Stay here. You promised that you'd stay."

"I cannot, I cannot leave my ship."

"Won't you sacrifice an imaginary duty for my love?"

"I cannot, Virginia, I cannot."

"Oh, I hate you."

6

He shrank as though someone had struck him in the face. "Virginia," he said, solemnly, "I hope I shall be killed in that battle."

"No, no, no, forgive me. I did not mean it; oh, I love you, Earl, my Earl!" For the first time in his life he saw Virginia cry—great sobs like a man's—deep—convulsing her whole body, and she swayed forward, helpless, in his arms.

From the bay came the roar of a hundred guns—dreadful—filling the world.

CHAPTER VII.

THE MERRIMAC.

Before the battle opened, General von Benzinger, having given orders for the establishment of his troops on the picket line, had ridden down to the shore. He sat calmly on his black horse and awaited the slow approach of the Merrimac. He watched the excitement of the soldiers in Camp Butler, the hurried preparations of the artillerymen of the Newport News battery. He watched the great ram draw near, while cannon-balls from ship and shore glanced like harmless hail from her slanting sides of iron. He watched her beak plow through the side of the Cumberland, and saw the gallant sloop go down with cheering crew and blazing guns and flying flags.

The Cumberland sunk, the Merrimac turned ponderously, sending her great shells crashing into the shore batteries. Then she made for the Congress, whose pilot had run her hard aground on Hampton bar. It was slow, methodical, merciless. The good ship was raked, shattered, set afire, and half her crew shot down without being able to bring a gun to bear. Having dispatched her second victim, the Merrimac turned imperturbably eastward to the Minnesota, hard aground, even as the Congress. Beyond her were the Roanoke and St. Lawrence, also hard aground. The Federal fleet could neither fight nor run. Von Benzinger observed the peculiar piloting, but alone of all the men on shore and sea he showed no excitement, made no movement, gave no sign. The Merrimac's shells now fell upon the Minnesota.

Under the frigate's lofty rail a little steamer, like a frightened fawn, had taken refuge from the Merrimac. From shore put out a large skiff, rowed rapidly by a single man. As the skiff neared the frigate, one of the Merrimac's shells struck the little steamer. Her boiler exploded, tearing her almost in two, killing and wounding several of her men. Fragments of iron knocked splinters from the side of the Minnesota. The little steamer sank almost immediately, her crew leaping to avoid the suction of her plunge. Shells screamed and burst. The man in the skiff rowed about picking up the survivors, one—two—three—four, and then a man

The Merrimac.

evidently more dead than alive. The crew of the Minnesota cheered as the man from the skiff took the wounded sailor in his arms and carried him up the ladder to the deck. Not far behind Von Benzinger a dismounted artillery subaltern was watching the incident.

"Hanged if that isn't the cool chap who took my horse!" exclaimed the subaltern. "What has he done with my horse?"

"By Jimtown," drawled a newspaper correspondent, who came up just in time to see the man from the boat. "That's Earl Hamilton! Won't he be sore?"

"Earl Hamilton, is it?" grunted the subaltern. "I wish he'd bring my horse back. Why will he be sore?"

"Three months ago he hired these cussed pilots for the fleet. Look at 'em now!" Every Federal ship in the Roads was at that moment aground.

General von Benzinger seemed to pay no attention to this talk. But he listened keenly, and noted, for possible use, the name of Earl Hamilton—the man who hired the pilots.

Willis caught sight of Von Benzinger and lowered his voice. "What's *he* doing here?" The newspaper man had the simon-pure American's usually unjustifiable distrust of a well-bred foreigner.

"Looking on, I suppose," said the subaltern. "That's about all anybody can do," he added, ruefully. "That damned turtle don't care how much you pitch shot at her. Look at those fool infantrymen up there shooting musket balls at her."

"His command's back on the picket line facing Magruder," said Willis, observing without comment the "fool infantrymen."

"His?" grinned the subaltern, indicating the General. "You better tell him so." To the subaltern it was beyond human audacity to address a brigadier unless he spoke first. Willis was different.

"I say, General," he called out, "what are you doing down here?"

Von Benzinger looked for an instant at Willis as though he were not going to answer. Then his lips curled with a trace of scorn, and he said, slowly:

"I have seen strange things, but never before now have I seen men shoot spit-balls at the hippopotamus."

"Good phrase, General, I'll print that. You should have been a newspaper man."

The dignified officer raised his shoulders, expressing lack of appreciation for the profession.

"I suppose you enjoy this sight about as much as the rest of us," added Willis, dolefully nodding at the bay.

"The North refused to build a Merrimac. She reaps what she has sown." Von Benzinger turned his horse away, as though the interview were distasteful. Then, turning back with a new thought, he said, more cordially, "Do you happen to know who that fine fellow is who rescued those men in the water?"

Willis was, habitually, more willing to gather than to give information, but he judged it well to atone for his familiarity with the General.

"That's Hamilton," he said, "Lieutenant Hamilton, on the Minnesota—a Southerner true to the Union."

"I met the Minnesota's officers," said Von Benzinger, "and he was not among them."

"Been in the Charleston flotilla the last three months. He's back just in time to be slaughtered by the Merrimac."

"Thanks to his Government's blindness," said Von Benzinger, his face darkening and his voice pitiless. Then, realizing that he had been a trifle indiscreet, he added, "I feel that if the Government had listened to me, we would long ago have had a

Merrimac, and this"—he swept his hand across the scene of the sea fight—"this disaster would never have occurred."

Having skillfully obtained a bit of information that interested him, Von Benzinger bade Willis a rather curt "good day," and rode off.

"The spiteful old devil acts as though he were glad of the Merrimac's work," observed Willis to the subaltern.

"He simply resented your manner of addressing him," replied the scandalized young officer.

"He didn't seem flattered," admitted Willis. "But he's a crank on iron ships and this gives him a chance to say, 'I told you so.'"

The Merrimac, during this colloquy, had been pounding the Minnesota at long range. She was keeping out of the shoal water in the north channel, which had proved so disastrous to the Union ships. Finally, about five o'clock, deciding that she could do her work better at high tide tomorrow, she turned slowly back to Norfolk. She had destroyed, that afternoon, two ships and near four hundred men, and the worst of it was, she had demonstrated her power to destroy, single-handed, the whole wooden navy of the North. That night it seemed that nothing could harm, and nothing resist, the iron-sheathed ram. Today the Congress and the Cumberland, tomorrow the Minnesota, the Roanoke and St. Lawrence. Wood was at the mercy of iron, the Union was at the mercy of the Confederacy. Heroism, of which there had been plenty, could not overcome the odds. Before the Merrimac, men died and ships went down in vain. That night the sailors knew it was in vain, the watching thousands knew. By means of telegram and bulletin, the South knew and exulted, the North knew and despaired. In Richmond, Mallory and Davis; in Washington, Welles and Lincoln learned—with how different emotions—that the control of the sea had passed from North to South. The Merrimac could sink ships, pass batteries, raise the blockade of all Confederate ports, bombard or levy tribute on every Northern sea-port, and, if she chose, lay Washington in ashes. Barges and canal boats full of stone were held in readiness to obstruct, at a moment's notice, the path of the Merrimac up the Potomac. Huge guns were hastily mounted on the shore. The Governors of Maine, Massachusetts and New York were wired immediately to place heavy batteries behind great rafts of timber. The commandant of every Atlantic fort and earthwork was ordered to regard the enemy as being actually present in his front. No one knew where or when the terrible ship would strike, and all was panic. Men lost their heads. Stanton telegraphed Cornelius Vanderbilt, asking how much he would take to destroy the Merrimac—a queer instance of American reliance on the power of money. In Washington houses Senators and Cabinet officers sat together, deep into the night, conferring with engineers and experts. They listened, uneasily, at open windows, half expecting to hear, breaking the stillness, the thunder of the Merrimac's great guns. That one structure of wood and iron struck greater terror to the nation's heart than all the power of Johnston's victorious regiments at Bull Run.

When the low tide stopped at last the carnage of that day, when the rack and ruin was over, and the Merrimac, leaving till the morrow her certain prey, steamed quietly back to Norfolk, then General von Benzinger turned serenely from the shore and rode up through the woods to Waverley.

CHAPTER VIII.

THE MASK.

When Von Benzinger arrived at his newly established headquarters, near Waverley, he found the senior colonel of his brigade in a great state of agitation. During the sea fight, a Confederate line of battle had advanced within a thousand yards of the Union pickets, which were only a mile and a half back of Newport News, thus bringing Waverley between the opposing lines. The Colonel believed that Magruder was about to throw his whole force upon the most advanced regiment, in a land co-operation with the Merrimac's attack upon Newport News. Consequently, he was hurrying another regiment from its camp on the slope of the hill to the picket line back over the crest. One battalion had already passed through the fields of Waverley, in line of battle, and another was marching in column past the house. Von Benzinger sent staff officers flying with angry orders to the nervous Colonel.

"Tell Colonel Middleton to march that regiment back and give it its supper," he said. To that crestfallen officer's explanation of the danger and the necessity of meeting it, Von Benzinger replied, decisively, "Magruder will not attack. Let him alone."

"But he's there already—in line of battle," protested the Colonel.

"He has four thousand men to our twelve. He must hold two roads ten miles apart. He will not attack."

"Then why, in the name of goodness, don't we attack?" exclaimed the Colonel.

"That, if you wish, you may ask General Wool. Or," he added, with stinging sweetness, "you might telegraph McClellan."

The Colonel subsided and went to his regiment. The General's tent being already set up, he dismounted, and turned Thetis over to his "striker," or "dog-robber"—the names given by the men to an officer's personal servant. The cook and kitchen police, undisturbed by the rumors of impending battle, were preparing supper for the General and his staff. Three orderlies were playing cards on an army blanket not far from the tent door. They had come to attention and saluted when the General appeared, and upon his acknowledgment, had gone back to their game. The General did not notice it, for he had learned to accommodate himself to the comparatively free and easy ways of American soldiering. He threw himself upon the grass and luxuriated for a moment in the relaxation from his long-maintained position on horseback. From the still burning frigate in the bay, and the battle whose result contained so much personal satisfaction for him, his thoughts came back to the house at Waverley, whose red-roofed stone towers showed amid the tree tops on the hill. The image of Virginia, as he had seen her that morning, came back into his mind with an exquisite shock. Entertaining the image for a moment, a new thought struck him, and he said to himself, "Why not?"

"Orderly," he called. The three youths leaped up, dropping their cards in confusion on the blanket. "You will come with me," he said, picking the best looking one, "and you," addressing the others, "will give my compliments to Captain Geary and tell him I've gone to Waverley—the house on the hill. Also that my headquarters may, perhaps, be moved there immediately after supper."

The General soon appeared at Waverley, where he found Mrs. Poynter, the Squire, and the darkies greatly excited over the marching and countermarching of the Union troops, and the rumors that there was to be a battle with the Confederates "right in our back yard," as Mrs. Poynter had it. Von Benzinger reassured them as to the danger of a battle, explaining that had he himself been present, the alarming demonstrations would never have occurred.

"You dear, good, considerate thing," said Mrs. Poynter, enthusiastically. "I might have known you were too polite to have a battle here, where we'd be killed. And so you stopped it! I do believe you can do anything, General von Benzinger, and I'm very grateful to you, and"—she added, seeing the General's eyes wandering into the house—"I'm sure Virginia will be, too, poor dear."

"I regret that you were alarmed. It was so needless," said the General, who was not unwilling, however, to have credit for saving Waverley from fire and sword.

"You are a Federal General, sah," said Squire Henderson, mopping his brow; "you are a Federal General, and yet, sah, I agree with you. The alarm of the ladies was certainly exaggerated."

"How about your own, Squire?" asked Mrs. Poynter.

"My alarm, Mrs. Poynter! My alarm? I may lack the physical vigoh, ma'am, to resist invaders on the field of battle, but I told you, Mrs. Poyntah, that life an' prop'rty 'd be a mighty sight safah if the Yankees were driven from the soil of this peninsula." Having given this indisputable proof of his valor, the Squire looked anxiously at the General to see if he were offended. Von Benzinger, however, was impatiently waiting for him to finish his speech.

"Is Miss Eggleston to be seen?" he asked.

"I'll call her, General; come in."

"Whah's Joe?" said the Squire. "I declare, Mrs. Poyntah, if you'll excuse me, I'll have to hunt up that niggah o' mine."

Mrs. Poynter, having already entered the house without a word to the old fellow, we may safely assume that she was willing to excuse him. Von Benzinger, leaving his orderly outside, followed Mrs. Poynter into the library, in the west corner of the house. He was struck by the rich suits of steel armor standing with spear and shield, like guardians of the big hall. "Judge Eggleston's mediaevalism seems genuine," thought Von Benzinger; and the dark old tapestries which covered the library wall above the bookcases confirmed the thought. The last level ray of the sunlight through the northwest window, fell on a huntsman spiritedly winding his horn to his hounds amid the woods, a lady hawking, and a four-towered castle, which might almost have been Waverley itself, except for moat and bridge. Von Benzinger, waiting for Miss Eggleston, divined that here, in the Virginia of '62, more than anywhere else in the world, was preserved the provincial spirit of feudalism, a late imitation, at least, of the life of knight and lady. Even the ridiculous old Squire had a touch of the manner. And, mingling in his own veins the blood of noble and peasant, the thing appealed to Von Benzinger.

Virginia was upstairs, in her room, of which the windows gave views upon the Roads. Since noon she had lived months—before tomorrow's sunset she was to live years. Her love for Earl Hamilton had flamed up in full force and consciousness, kindling her whole nature, showing her that her father's wish, her love of country, must, whether she would or no, take second place within her heart. And he, loving her as she knew he did, even when she brought the full power of her love and will to bear upon him, was still unshakable inflexible as steel, and true to honor. Yes, honor was a thing he loved more than he loved her, and when she found it so, she loved him more—yes, more than honor.

And yet, the dreadful battle! Hour by hour she watched the fearful odds work out the merciless result. The Cumberland sunk, the Congress set afire, she saw, with agony, the great shells crash into the Minnesota—his ship—whither he had gone out of her arms, nor could Love hold him back.

Mrs. Poynter had come to her door and told her of the imminent battle about the house.

"I do not care, I do not care," she moaned, and refused to unlock the door. The fate of the other ships had caused her to abandon all hope that the Minnesota or Earl would be spared. The Merrimac was freeing her country and tearing her heart.

But when the Merrimac drew off, and the Minnesota, unlike the other ships, was not destroyed, Virginia's hopes revived, and she had hurried one of the negroes off to learn of her lover's fate.

As Mrs. Poynter stepped into the hall from the library, where she had left Von Benzinger, her vision passed through the arch into the parlor and out upon the southeast gallery. A man was just ascending the steps. Mrs. Poynter went quickly into the parlor and out through the French window. It was an oysterman sent up by Hamilton, after the battle, with a line telling Virginia he was unhurt.

"Bless the dear fellow's heart," thought Mrs. Poynter. "It will be like pardon to a woman condemned." She flew up the stairs to Virginia's room, shouting "good news" at the top of her lungs. This time the door opened with alacrity, and when Virginia's eyes had caught the welcome words that told her Earl was safe, she—well, she was all unstrung, and very happy, and forgot entirely for the moment that the battle would begin again tomorrow.

Then Mrs. Poynter told her that General von Benzinger had come back from the bay, and he had countermanded the battle at Waverley, and everything was perfectly lovely, and he was waiting down stairs to see her. A few moments later, with the quick rebound of her elastic spirits, a radiant Virginia greeted Von Benzinger.

"Ah, Miss Eggleston," he said, smiling, as Virginia gave him her hand. "I take it that Mrs. Poynter has relieved your anxiety as to the battle about your house."

"Oh, yes. And did you really, as she said, countermand the battle?" Virginia laughed musically at the absurd phrase.

"I simply countermanded some orders which might have made us blunder into a foolish skirmish."

"How lucky for us that you came! And this morning, too," she said, with seriousness. "That really placed us deeply in your debt—so deeply that we can never repay you."

"Ah, easily," he answered.

"May I ask how? Anything we can do, I'm sure—"

"Chiefly, Miss Eggleston, by letting me talk to you." A discreet cough announced Mrs. Poynter descending the stairs.

"Oh, that wouldn't do it. I'm sure you can think of better payment than that," answered Virginia.

"General von Benzinger," said Mrs. Poynter, entering, "when you went over that wall this morning you were the most beautiful thing I ever laid eyes on."

"Dear me," said Virginia, "you'll make the General vain. Of course he was, but you mustn't tell him so. And what a beautiful horse!"

"Will you accept the horse, Miss Eggleston?" he asked, quickly.

"Your horse?" she said, surprised. "Why, I could not do that."

"No, she couldn't accept it, General," said Mrs. Poynter, quickly, "but I'm sure it was very gallant of you to offer it. Our customs, you know—we all bow to Mrs. Grundy." Mrs. Poynter felt that the foreign gentleman might not understand the girl's scruple, and, in her pell-mell fashion, rushed the conversation on past the embarrassing point. She saved the situation, and soon had them both talking of other things.

"Do you live in a tent, too," she asked, presently.

"Yes," he said. "But, oddly enough, before I met you ladies this morning, I had decided to live in this house."

"That *is* a compliment!" exclaimed Mrs. Poynter. "*After* you met us, I suppose, you preferred to live in a leaky old tent."

"After I met you, I would not intrude myself, unbidden, upon people who had charmed me."

"Neat, General, neat. Well, do come and sleep in a dry room. Mayn't he, Virginia?"

"You do not understand, Mrs. Poynter," said he, quickly. "I intended to make my headquarters here, and bring with me my staff."

"Your whole staff!" exclaimed Mrs. Poynter. "Delightful!"

Virginia seconded Mrs. Poynter's invitation. She really wanted neither the Union General nor his staff, and she knew very well that her father didn't want them there at Waverley. She was under great obligations to Von Benzinger, however, and his delicacy in so quickly giving her a chance to withdraw, gracefully, Mrs. Poynter's invitation appealed to her. Of course he had the power simply to come without her permission. It was much better, if he was to be there, to be on decent terms with him.

So the General sent his orderly back to Captain Geary, his adjutant, instructing him to move the brigade headquarters to Waverley after supper. The General dined with Mrs. Poynter, Miss Eggleston, and the Squire. More and more, Von Benzinger was fascinated by this girl, whose personality, possessing the healthful freshness of the woods and fields, was yet instinct with the gracious manners and high spirit of a courtly old tradition. The man had no intimates in this country—he was here with a purpose, and since his arrival, a year before, he had spoken scarce ten words without a purpose. But now the ladies drew him out and he talked for talk's sake—incidents of battle and siege and storm at sea, shifting the scene from sweltering iron mills to the blithe dens of Parisian students; and, finally, he told them of La Gloire—the French ironclad which the Merrimac, he said, could easily crush. Few men could draw upon the experience of so many kinds of life; few men could be so interesting. Yet, as Virginia watched the free play of his expressive face and hands and shoulders, which, until now, she had seen severely controlled, as she saw his black eyes light up beneath his white, lustrous hair, and heard his sardonic humor as of a man who had fought the world bitterly, she felt as though the rigid soldier of the morning had dropped a mask. Was this really his face which he showed them now—was this the real man? Or, was it another mask?

CHAPTER IX.

THE PILOTS.

The sun had set an hour ago on the waters and shores of Hampton Roads, but they were not dark. The frigate Congress still burned fiercely in the bay. Her spars and cordage gleamed, clear-cut, in firelight; her square port holes glowed dark-red in her black hull; waves of flame surged up out of her hatches, and burnt through her decks, sweeping dense showers of sparks up toward the sky. The red light of that burning tinged the slightly rocking waters of the Roads, gleamed on the projecting masts and flying flags of the Cumberland, lighted the white tents of Camp Butler, made lurid the smoke-hung sky, and cast a dull glare on the window-panes of Waverley. In that strange light, the sea and shore and sky were weird as in a dream. Through the Federal camps, soldiers sat, moodily silent; to them the reddened world was colored with disaster. From Waverley they saw, far over toward Norfolk, the silent, momentary rise and arch of rockets against the distant sky. Had they been within hearing of those rockets' hiss, they would have found a people drunk with joy—celebrating the overwhelming victory of the Merrimac. From Michigan to Florida it was the same story—every mind in the country was turned with terror or delight to that red spot on the Atlantic coast where the Merrimac had half drawn out the cork of the Confederate bottle.

In Hampton Roads was the focus of all the mighty waves of emotion sweeping that night over the country; the news was flashed from town to town and passed from lip to lip, till every thought of North and South was turned intensely upon this one place, and it became the center of a spiritual storm—the core of a cyclone of hope and fear.

The fire had raged in the frigate since three that afternoon. All through the evening, on into the night, steadily the flames approached the magazines. At Waverley, the while the great ship burned, love and hate, suspicion, treason, guilt, and fear were likewise working toward a great disaster.

Soon after dark, Waterloo Willis came up the road from the new camp, and, turning in at an angle of the stone wall, approached the gate leading into the grounds of Waverley. As he did so, a sentinel, pacing his post along the slope, halted, brought his musket to charge, and cried, "Who goes there?"

"Your affectionate friend," replied the Yankee, stopping to light a fresh cigar.

"Advance, friend, and give the countersign."

Approaching to within a few feet of the guard, Willis stretched forward one of his long arms, flipped the ashes from his cigar along the shining steel of the bayonet, and said, in his cool, drawling fashion, "Virginia."

"Fair," replied the guard.

"Rebel," responded the correspondent.

"The countersign is right. Pass on," and the sentinel, throwing his gun carelessly across his shoulder, continued on his rounds.

"Virginia, fair rebel," repeated Willis, advancing up the carriage road and turning into the path that led to the house. "Von Benzinger's countersign is significant. I wonder if Miss Eggleston is pleased with the compliment."

"Hello, Waterloo. Glad to see you. Rather busy day all 'round, eh?"

The speaker, Captain Geary, was a short, compactly built man, of perhaps fifty, with close-cropped gray hair and beard, and a florid complexion.

"Right you are, Captain. The Merrimac has worked destruction in the Roads today."

"Yes, devil take her. You can see the Cumberland's flag from here. Have a look?" he continued, offering Willis the glass through which he had been scanning the harbor.

"Obliged to you, Captain, but I haven't the heart. That flag marks the grave of as brave a company of men as ever died for a just cause."

"Not a man surrendered," exclaimed the adjutant, with military pride. "They fought their guns to the water's edge and went down with their colors flying."

"I sympathize with yo', gentlemen," said Henderson, coming forward from a shadow of the wall, polishing his bald head with his big bandanna. "Yo' Yankees did, indeed, fight like heroes; but the prejudice of a co'respondent has led you into an error, Mr. Willis. Ours is the just cause, sah, according to the constitution, conceived and established by that noble Virginian and sublime patriot, George Washington, sah."

"Eloquent, Squire," replied Willis, with a cold smile, "but, by Jimtown, did it ever occur to you that things have changed somewhat in the last century, constitutions included?"

"They have never changed where the rights of

prope'ty are consa'ned, sah, not since Adam took possession of the brute creation, sah, an' named 'em, an' set 'em to wu'k fo' him, sah. Wondah wha' that black rascal, Joe, is," he said, suddenly dropping his rhetorical style and looking anxiously about. "I can't heah of him anywha'. Nevah knew him to leave me befo'. Ef yo' Yankee soldiers have stolen that niggah, Cap'n, I'll—"

"Don't be alarmed, Henderson," said Geary, winking broadly at Willis; "your property will turn up all right. There isn't a Yankee recruit mean enough to take the last prop from the house of a Southern gentleman who knows how to mix a morning drink and reveres the constitution, eh, Willis?"

"By Jimtown, Geary, I wouldn't have the Squire and Joe separated for a New England homestead," said Willis, puffing furiously at his weed. "When 'd you miss him, Squire?"

" 'Bout half an hour ago, sah. I went in thar to protest to the General about takin' this house fo' his headquarters, an' in the excitement of my hurried departure I fo'got all about the niggah, sah. An' I hain't been able to locate him since. Heah, yo', Joe!" he cried, turning suddenly and shouting into the garden.

"Might call the corporal of the guard, Captain,

and order a search," said Willis, half in earnest. "If that boy isn't returned to the Squire, I shall be up a stump for amusement."

"If I find a damned Yankee soldier tryin' to run that boy off, I'll shoot him on sight," proclaimed the Squire, going up the steps.

"And you'd be justified by the constitution, Squire. I'm with you on that proposition," Willis called after him.

In the doorway the Squire halted, took out his handkerchief, removed his hat, and rubbed the smooth surface of his head, slowly. Having thus refreshed his memory, he retraced his steps to the center of the gallery.

"The print I brought this morning from Little Bethel, an' which I allowed yo' to read, Mr. Willis," he said, with an awkward attempt not to soar, "cannot be found, sah. A Richmond papah is a luxury in these times, sah. Ef either of yo' gentlemen can give me any information concerning it, I should deem it a favor."

"I was interested in it myself, Squire. Did you ask Estelle? She was with us at the time, I remember." Willis was feeling his way cautiously.

"Yes, sah. She tol' me she laid it away somewha' but the exact place has slipped her recollection, sah.

I wondah wha' that niggah Joe is?" he said, the lesser loss suggesting the greater.

"Hang Joe," growled Geary, with a shrug.

"Captain Geary!" cried the Squire, red anger flushing his face.

"Only a suggestion, Squire. You don't need to follow it, at least not until you find the boy. Why don't you tell your troubles to Mrs. Poynter. She might be able to help you."

"Your latter suggestion redeems the fo'mah," said the Squire, resuming his natural pompous manner. "Mrs. Poynter is a superior woman, sah. I will endeavor to find her."

"Be careful not to get into the General's room," cried Willis. But the Squire was out of hearing.

"He's safe enough if he does," said Geary. "The General isn't there."

"Where is he?" Willis inquired, with more interest than he usually displayed.

"He went out a while ago to inspect the picket lines. That's military training, Willis. All the details in hand and nothing trusted to subordinates."

"If training will make a general, Von Benzinger's chances are away up, I reckon," replied Willis with a queer ring in his drawl. "By the way, Geary, have you heard any more about the grounding of the ships? There seems to be a big suspicion that all the pilots were bought up in anticipation of the attack, and that the ships were run on the shoals to give the Merrimac a cock-sure chance to destroy 'em."

"It looks that way. When Von Benzinger came back from watching the fight, he told me that a Union naval lieutenant, named Hamilton, had recommended the pilots in the first place, that he was a Southerner born and bred, and that he was under suspicion. Do you know the fellow?"

"Hamilton! Hamilton!" repeated Willis, slowly. "Never heard of him." He was startled to hear his own words of sympathy for Hamilton spoken that afternoon, being used to fasten suspicion on his friend. There was something uncanny about it.

"And so Von Benzinger thinks Hamilton's the man," he said, half aloud. "That's queer."

"What's queer. That Von Benzinger—"

"That the men bobbing around in that boat out there don't get raised out of the water with a shell from some quarter—Federal or Confederate," he drawled, not wishing Geary to suspect the trend of his thought. "Ha, they're turning straight for the mouth of the Elizabeth. Your glass again, Geary!"

"All right; keep it till I return from a tramp through camp. General's orders. Anything startling in the boat?" he continued, as Willis lowered the glasses.

"Oystermen," said Willis, sententiously.

"Nothing worth a headline in that," laughed the Captain. "Gad, you newspaper men would find something suspicious in the changing features of the moon."

"Which is about to take a look at the world on its own account," said Willis, jerking the glasses at a silvery rim just beginning to show along the eastern horizon.

"And I suppose you'll hang around here to enjoy its mellow light in company with the gay Washington widow. She seems to be leading you and the Squire a very pretty chase." And the bluff, grizzled Captain chuckled immoderately.

"I cannot agree with you, Mrs. Poynter." It was the Squire's voice raised in the usual protest.

"Here they come. Brace yourself for the chase, old fellow. The Squire has the constitution on his side, but you have the power of the press behind you, which makes it an even fight. I'm off. My regards to the widow." And the Captain, adjusting his sword belt, threw back his shoulders and swung down the path toward the line of white tents showing dimly in the distance.

"Oh, there you are, Waterloo," said Mrs. Poynter,

running lightly down the steps. "You truant, where have you been all afternoon. I've been dying for some one who had a thought above the Confederacy to sympathize with me over the fate of those beautiful ships! That iron monster! Isn't it a shame?"

"Sank the Cumberland, bu'ned the Congress, an' began on the Minnesota," declaimed the Squire, converting the gallery into a rostrum. "The iron monster to which you refer, Mrs. Poynter, has saved the menaced property of this peninsula." Then suddenly feeling about for Joe and not finding him, the Squire broke down, and, more from habit than with any hope of answer, he added, "Wha's Joe?"

"Squire Henderson, if I were a man—" began the widow, indignantly.

"Were you a man, Mrs. Poynter," interrupted Willis, "you would be in danger of the draft."

"And we should be in danger of losing a most charming companion," added the Squire, with a deep bow, his gallantry getting the better of his anxiety about his lost property.

"Squire, you are a flatterer," said the widow, tapping him lightly with her fan.

"A flatterer, Mrs. Poynter?" drawled Willis, with a surprised inflection.

"Yes, and I'm angry at being praised on account of my sex."

"Is that because you are of that sex?" said Willis, with a merry twinkle in his blue eyes. "I had supposed that in the eye of Vanity there was nothing worth while that did not reflect herself."

"By that you mean all women are vain."

"And all men industrious. Yes, something like that."

"Well, if industry is the chief of virtues, then the devil must be the chief of saints," cried Mrs. Poynter.

"The lady is eminently right, sah," interjected the Squire, crowding between Willis and the widow. "The northe'n idea that a man is mo' honorable because he makes his own co'n is a fallacy, sah. A puritan fallacy."

"By the same token, a man in the South should be more highly respected for making his own whiskey. Is that your argument, Squire?"

"The thoughtless are pleased with the tinkling of their own tongues, but the thoughtful are silent lest they utter indiscretions," laughed the widow. "But here comes the General's aide. Perhaps he brings news."

"Hallo, Edwards," called Waterloo, as the aide came up. "Know anything worth while?"

"Know 't the road from here to the fort's ankle deep in dust an' mighty slow ridin'.""

"What's the latest gossip about headquarters?"

"Everybody talkin' 'bout the treachery o' the pilots who ran the ships aground."

"Think it was planned?"

"Bet your life it was. Bribery an' nothing else."

"Any arrests?"

"Not yet. Department keepin' everything dark, I guess."

"Any clew to who did the bribing?"

"Not that I heard. Must have been someone on our side though. If he's caught I pity him," growled the weary aide, climbing the steps and entering the door that led to Von Benzinger's quarters.

"What's this about the pilots and treachery, Waterloo? I declare you are close mouthed as the sphinx. I suppose every general in the Union army might turn traitor and I should have to wait for some common soldier to come along and give me the news. Squire, I take back all I said this morning about Washington courtesy." Mrs. Poynter's tone was quite severe. "Willis is the most selfish man of my acquaintance. Let's go look for Joe!" and taking the Squire's arm she sailed away, her light, fluffy hair shining in the moonlight like finely spun gold.

The correspondent watched them as they passed down the winding path toward the wood, the widow's tall, well-proportioned figure and easy, graceful movements contrasting strongly with the short, corpulent figure of the Squire, who rose on his toes after each step in an evident endeavor to reach that altitude in the world to which his egotism had exalted him.

"She's handsome," was the correspondent's mental comment. "I wonder if she's as heartless as she pretends. Hello," he ejaculated aloud, "I thought you'd gone."

Lafe Harlan had come suddenly around an angle of the house. Upon seeing Willis, he stopped, took off his wide-brimmed, black beaver hat, and threw back his hair with a jerk of his head.

"It isn't my fault that I'm here," he said. "I'd have been on the other side o' the James this morning if some o' your damned Yankee soldiers hadn't caught sight o' me and come near capturing me."

"How do you come to be walking about here inside the Union lines, and under the nose of a Union general?"

"Because I have permission from the General himself."

"General von Benzinger?"

"You heard what I said."

"But does he know who you are?"

"Ask him, if you're anxious to know."

"By Jimtown, if I understand it." And Willis planted his feet wide apart, shoved his hands up to the wrists in his pockets, and stood looking at Harlan. "How'd you work it?" he said, after a pause. The guerrilla's audacity pleased him.

"Result of circumstances. Yanks chase me in here, surround the house, overpower me, and are about to drag me away when the General rides up, and in response to a request from my pretty cousin, orders the Yanks to release me. Being protected, I've stayed. That's clear, ain't it?"

"Well, what about the paper. Suppose I show it to Miss Eggleston?"

"You won't, because you haven't got it to show."

The two men eyed each other, measuring their advantages and disadvantages as men try their rapiers before a duel.

"See here," Harlan said, suddenly. "There's no reason why we should quarrel. I have made up my mind to leave here at the first opportunity. Whatever your plans are, you don't want to turn me over to the Yanks or you'd a done it before this. Now, you promise to keep mum about that paper, an' I'll give Hamilton a free field with Virginia. Is it a bargain?"

"Go ahead," said Willis, after a pause. "I'll trust you that far. But don't make it necessary for me to call on General Wool."

Harlan took off his hat, shook the hair out of his eyes, gave Willis a sharp glance, and turning about walked toward the stone archway leading to the stable. As he turned the corner of the wall he looked back over his shoulder and called, "When you find that paper let me know."

"I wonder if the girl gave him the paper, or is keeping it herself for some reason of her own," thought Willis. I don't believe Harlan's sure about it, or he wouldn't be so friendly. If it wasn't for Hamilton's squeamishness about having an old playmate hanged as a spy, I'd make short work of him. I wonder if Von Benzinger suspects what a rich prize his gallantry is letting slip through his fingers? This foreign General is a puzzle to me. What motive induced him to twist my reference to Hamilton and the pilots into a suspicion? By Jimtown, I'm getting as loquacious as an old maid at a tea party. If anything should happen to that fine young lieutenant through my silly speech, I should feel like blowing my brains out."

Friendship had sprung up between Willis and

Hamilton almost at their first meeting. They were as different in manner, speech and action as it was possible for two men to be, but both were honest and brave to rashness, and they trusted each other implicitly.

"I must see Miss Eggleston and tell her of this new danger to Hamilton," was Willis' final decision. Just as he was about to carry his thought into execution, Geary returned from the camps, and together they entered the house. In the hall they met Virginia. A light wrap was thrown about her shoulders and she carried her hat on her arm.

"How do you do, Mr. Willis," she said, giving him her hand. "I was just going to look for Mrs. Poynter. The house seems so still and lonely after the roar of the guns. I have often felt I should like to go to war for my country, but today's experiences have satisfied me. I hope never to repeat them."

"And I hope you never may. Captain, if you'll excuse me, I will remain for a word with Miss Eggleston. With your permission, of course," he continued, bowing to Virginia.

"Certainly," said Virginia, smiling graciously.

"You'll find me in the first room to the left, off the hall," said the Captain. "Drop in before you go."

"I thought perhaps you might wish to hear of Hamilton," said Waterloo, when they were alone, rightly guessing where her thoughts lay.

"I have been told that he was not hurt in the battle."

"Not in the battle, no, Miss Eggleston."

"What do you mean," she said, growing pale at the thought his words suggested.

"I mean, Miss Eggleston, that Earl Hamilton is in great danger; a danger that threatens not only his life, but what is dearer to him than life—his honor."

"Tell me what you mean."

"You know the Union ships were run aground?"

"Yes."

"And the pilots are believed to have been bribed?"

"I have heard something of it."

"Hamilton hired these men some weeks ago."

"Because he knew them."

"That's it exactly, and because he did hire them, because he knew them, and because he is a Virginian, they say—"

"Not that he has played false to the Union."

"Yes."

"It isn't true!"

Before her rose the picture of that morning in the

garden, when not for her love would he think a disloyal thought.

"It isn't true!" she said again, her eyes shining like stars. "Who dares charge him with treachery?"

"No one directly, but I learned since I came here that Von Benzinger had spoken of it."

"General von Benzinger! What does he know of Earl Hamilton?"

"He does not know him, and, what is more important, he doesn't know that you know him."

"Why should that concern him?"

"It doesn't. Listen. I have as much faith in Hamilton's integrity as you have. But it is important we should be aware of who is behind this charge. I don't know that Von Benzinger knows any more about it than we do. I don't know that he does not know all about it. It is important that we should find out without raising his suspicions. You can do this, and you alone."

"I? In what way?"

"Draw him into conversation. Be careful not to mention Hamilton's name nor suggest that suspicion rests on him. The General is vain—as we all are—and may tell you something that will help us. The country is greatly excited. Such a thing as a fair trial for a man once accused of grounding the ships would be out of the question. It must never be made if Hamilton is innocent—as he is," Willis hastened to say, seeing the fire gathering in her eyes. "Will you help me?"

Virginia stood for a moment looking through the door at the burning ships. A sudden kindling in the sails threw a light, like a halo, over her dark hair. "You may depend on me," she said, looking Willis squarely in the eyes.

"You're worthy of him. Thank you," said Willis, simply. Then he strode away to the room indicated by Geary.

CHAPTER X.

THE WHITE SLAVE.

While the events which meant so much to the nation were crowding one another in quick succession in all that part of Virginia, Estelle had hidden herself in her room, clinging to the paper brought by the Squire. The paragraph in which five thousand dollars reward was offered for Lafe Harlan fascinated her. It had for her a power greater than anything of which she had ever dreamed. At the first mention of it, Harlan had run away from an unarmed man. This small piece of printed white paper was more feared by him than sword or pistol. Without knowing it, she recognized the force of type and bowed down to it and worshiped it.

When Estelle fled from Willis to hide the paper, it was to her no more than a suggestion. In some remote way she felt that it gave her power over Harlan. It was a new fetish which appealed to the hereditary superstitions in her blood. If the mere mention of it by an unarmed adversary could cause obedience in the man whom she had believed to be brave beyond fear, why should the possession of it not in some way bring Harlan to think of her—to accept help from her. He was in danger; his life was sought on every hand. If she could plan his escape and they were to go away together, would he not be grateful? Somewhere beyond this roar of guns and smoke of battle there must be a place of peace where they might live without fear—where no one could question her right to love and happiness.

Having reasoned so far as this, she began to ask herself why it would not be an act of kindness to force Harlan to go away from Waverley. Here he would always be subject to his infatuation for Virginia, and while Estelle felt sure Virginia would never redeem her father's pledge by marrying Harlan, she knew that were he to remain here he would be lost to her forever. Over and over again since his return she had laid plans to help him to escape and to follow him wherever he might go, making herself so necessary to him, doing his will so blindly, that he would at last feel grateful and reward her with his love. But after the pursuit of the morning and his release by General von Benzinger at Virginia's request, she lost all hope. Then her thoughts reverted to the paper. Willis had said if it fell into Virginia's hand she would despise Harlan and drive him from her roof. Why should it not be so. He was endangering his life in a vain suit for a hand that would never be his. Once beyond the sound of Virginia's voice, he would forget her.

All day these thoughts had chased each other through her brain. When night came and the sound of firing ceased, she crept up the stairs to her room, and taking the crumpled paper in her hands, sat down in the gloom, and rocking herself to and fro, sang softly to herself:

> "Wi' lightsome heart I pu'd a rose,
>   Fu' sweet upon its thorny tree;
> And my fause lover stole the rose,
>   But ah! he left the thorn for me."

At last she left the room, and groping her way to the stairs, went below, holding the paper tightly clasped in her hand, hoping, yet almost dreading, to meet Virginia. Her world was so small, this action meant so much to her! Suppose Lafe should hate her for what she was going to do. He must not know. Willis had threatened to tell Virginia. If she sent him away, Lafe would suspect the correspondent and not know that Estelle had disclosed the secret.

Now that the battle was over, the night seemed strangely still. The shrill staccato of a cricket sounded louder in her ears than had the roar of musketry, and the sudden call of a sentry shook her more than the roar of a battery had done. Some-one was moving along the gallery, and she recognized the voices of Virginia and Lafe. She slipped into the dining-room, crept near one of the windows, and listened. In the light from the burning ship she could see everything about the place as clearly as at noonday. Lafe and Virginia stood talking earnestly. They were looking toward the Roads, but she saw the man's face cut in sharp profile against the burning ship, and a great yearning stirred under her heart and thrilled her whole being. It was as if she had been baptized with a new and subtle essence. Her head swam with the mighty love that took possession of her. The world was swept aside, and there was nothing but that dark, wild face, framed in its mass of black hair flung carelessly away from the high, narrow forehead—the flash of the deep-set eyes, and in her heart that strange new love, which swept over and possessed her, and whispered to her soul a secret that is told only once in the world to a human being, and that being—a woman.

Dizzy with her emotions, Estelle groped blindly for support. Her hand fell on the sideboard, and her fingers closed over the barrel of one of the pistols Seth had prepared for Virginia's use. She took it from the case, and carrying it to the window, examined it critically by the light of the burning ship. She had often assisted Virginia in her target practice, and she saw now that the pistol was properly loaded and ready for action. She hesitated a moment, glanced through the window at the two forms outlined against the burning sky, and then concealing the weapon in the folds of her dress, she found her way to the hall and hurried up the stairs.

A few moments later, Virginia said good-night to Harlan and entered the house. On her way through the hall she passed the room now occupied by Von Benzinger. The door stood partly open, and she caught a glimpse of the interior as she went by. On a small table near the window burned a sperm oil lamp. The flickering flame sent strange shadows dancing in the recesses. Lying on the table were several bundles of papers neatly tied with tape. The General was absent, but Virginia seemed to see him sitting in the chair beside the table, on his face the same strange smile she had noticed at supper. Despite Von Benzinger's suave manners and courteous speech, she distrusted him, and fell to wondering what his past life had been and why he, an educated foreigner and soldier of renown, should be content to serve a stranger's country in so contracted a sphere.

These thoughts were still occupying her mind when she entered her room. She was surprised to find the candles already lighted and Estelle, with a feverish color in her cheeks, standing near the door in an attitude of expectancy.

"What's the matter, Estelle!" said Virginia, halting in the doorway, "are you ill? You look so much like a ghost, you startled me!"

"There ain't nuthin' the mattah with me, Miss Virginia," replied the girl, in a low, strained voice, and dropping into the negro dialect, as she always did when uncommonly moved or excited. "But tha's somethin' yo' ought to know. An' yet I don' like ter be the one ter tell yo'."

"Why, Estelle, what do you mean? If you know anything that concerns the welfare of anyone on this plantation, it is your duty to tell me What is it? Who is in trouble?"

"Lafe!" replied the girl, and there was such a wail of agony in the sound of the one spoken word that Virginia started and peered into the girl's face in wonderment.

"He's sold secrets of the Confederacy to the Yankees. The South has set a price on his head."

"Estelle, you are dreaming," said Virginia. "Lafe Harlan a Union spy! Who's been putting such nonsense into your head?"

"I heard the Washington man tell him so to his face this morning, and Lafe didn't kill him, but went away, as he was ordered, so I know it's true."

"This is some new Yankee trick. Lafe is out there on the gallery now. I'll go and ask him to explain."

"O, don't, Miss Virginia, don't tell him I told yo', fo' he would kill me." The girl threw herself on her knees. "Promise me yo' won't tell him I told you. Fo' God's sake, promise that an' I'll serve yo' all my life." The girl was sobbing convulsively. Virginia put her arms about Estelle and raised her to her feet.

"Don't be afraid," she said, soothingly. "I promise you Lafe shall never know you said a word about it. It can be nothing more than idle gossip anyway."

"Deed an' it ain't, Miss Virginia," cried the girl, gathering courage with the assurance that Lafe was not to know of her part in the transaction. "It's all in this papah the Squire brought from Little Bethel this morning. The stranger read it an' told

Lafe about it. I heard him, and saw the paper lyin' in the library wha' the man dropped it, an' brought it away. Here it is, an' yo' can read fo' yo'self."

Estelle picked up the paper from the table and gave it to Virginia. It was so folded that the head line proclaiming the reward for Harlan, dead or alive, for betraying secrets of the Confederacy, was the first thing Virginia saw. She read it through hurriedly at first and then slowly. Gradually the lines about the corner of her mouth deepened, her nostrils dilated, her shoulders stiffened, and a resolute light came into her eyes.

"Go to your room, Estelle," she said, without taking her eyes from the paragraph. "I shan't need you again tonight. Harlan shall never know how this came into my hands. You will be in no danger."

"And you will let him remain here?" inquired Estelle, with a fear that, after all, her exposure of Harlan's treachery might fail of its purpose.

"Remain here!" said Virginia, lifting her proud head. "A traitor to the South remain under this roof? Not if he were my own brother!"

Estelle's heart gave a great leap when she heard this, and slipping out, she ran to her room, caught up a small bundle in which she had already wrapped everything of value she possessed, threw a scarf

9

about her shoulders, secreted under it the bundle
and Virginia's pistol, which she had previously
brought from the dining-room, and going quietly
down a rear stairway, took a position in the shadow
of a tower near the wood that lay between the house
and the James River.

When Virginia bade Harlan good-night and left
him alone, he was in a pleasant frame of mind. The
early hours of the morning had been fraught with
danger and full of disagreeable adventures. His
meeting with Willis and the disclosures of the Richmond paper had made it impossible to remain longer
at Waverley. Should he disobey the injunctions of
Willis to go away, he knew the correspondent well
enough to feel sure Virginia would be made acquainted with his treachery, which thing he dreaded
above all others. Wild and reckless as he was, he
loved with a fierce, tiger passion this proud, high-
spirited girl. Her beauty, her high sense of honor,
her devotion to the South and her quick sympathies
aroused in him an admiration which he did not take
the trouble to analyze. Perhaps it was because the
virtues she possessed were entirely lacking in himself that he held them in such high regard. He
loved her and longed to possess her, with all the
fervor of a passionate nature that was a stranger to
control. But in her presence, the cavalier airs which

sat so easily on him at all other times deserted him, and the boastful words familiar to his speech stuck in his throat and failed of utterance. Had Lafe Harlan been born in Italy, he would have been a captain of brigands, reveling in the dangers of a lawless life. He was enough of an Arab to love his horse; enough of an American to handle a pistol with skill, and shoot with accuracy; enough of a robber to love money, and enough of a Gascon to throw it away with a great show of liberality when it was once in his possession. The war had given him the opportunity to indulge his propensities. Happening to be in Washington when the struggle began, he offered his services to General McClellan, and as he was well acquainted with the country in which operations were being carried on, and had a way of winning the confidence of his associates, he was employed to run between the lines and bring reports of the enemy's contemplated movements. Sometimes these reports were true, and sometimes not, according to his moods. It was while he was engaged in this work that he met Willis, and it was Willis who had detected Harlan's treachery to the Union. At that time Willis had laid plans for Harlan's exposure, but at Hamilton's request Willis simply warned Harlan to get out. Lafe fled to the Confederate lines, raised a company of guer-

rillas, and scoured the country between the opposing forces, laying tribute wherever opportunity offered or occasion demanded. Virginia was ignorant
of Harlan's earlier movements. Hamilton had naturally shrunk from saying anything that might
hint at enmity on his part. And so to her Lafe had
always been loyal to the South, and his company
of freebooters were in her eyes a party of brave
patriots pitted against a host of unrighteous invaders.

Harlan's arrest by the patrol in the morning, and
his subsequent release by Von Benzinger, placed
him at once beyond the fear of danger for the present. The publication of his treachery in the Richmond papers made it impossible to return to the
Southern lines, but he was quick-witted enough to
know that General von Benzinger had a motive in
protecting him, and while that motive remained he
felt himself secure. It was a single newspaper correspondent against a general of brigade, and the
odds were now all on his side.

"If I can keep that Richmond paper from falling
into Virginia's hands for a few days, I can snap my
fingers at all of them," he thought, going slowly into
the yard and crossing toward a clump of trees at the
edge of the knoll overlooking the James. "Judge
Eggleston is in Richmond, and he believes in me.

It will take more evidence than they can possibly have to convict me, if I can get there and give myself up without being shot for the reward. The Merrimac has changed the affairs on this peninsula, and nobody knows what will happen next."

He paced slowly back and forth in the shadows of the trees, swinging his arms slowly, his eyes bent on the ground.

"Lafe Harlan!"

The words, although spoken in a low tone, rang clear as a bell in the stillness. There was that in the sound of them that sent a shiver through the veins of Harlan, who threw up his head and turned abruptly. "Virginia," he said, and then stood still, he knew not why.

"Lafe Harlan," continued Virginia, standing straight as an arrow in the moonlight, and speaking in full, even tones, "you are my cousin and the son of my father's dearest friend. When I was yet a little girl I was taught to look upon you as my future husband. As we grew older and I saw how different we were in tastes and dispositions, I recognized the wickedness of such a union. But for the love I bore my father, and with a weakness which I now regret more than you can ever realize, I refrained from open disobedience to his wishes, hoping that you would at last look upon this union as I looked upon it, and release my father from his pledge. Nevertheless, when you came here a few days ago, flushed with victories in a cause I love better than life, you wore in my eyes the mantle of a hero. That mantle has fallen, and I know you to be neither hero nor man, but a traitor, who has betrayed the country in whose arms he was cradled, whose uniform he wears, and whose cause he has sworn to defend."

"Virginia—"

"Do not call me Virginia. I am nothing to you. Read that," she said, handing him the paper with his name in big, black type, clearly visible in the moonlight, "and then tell me why I should not call the slaves and have you thrown into the road."

Harlan took the paper from her hand, and glanced along the page. He had no need to read it, although this he could have done easily in the bright moonlight.

"It's a lie, Virginia! A damned Yankee lie!" he said, hoarsely.

"It is the truth. I know it. I feel it!" replied Virginia. "For the sake of your father's memory, I refrain from turning you over to be shot as you deserve, but if you are not beyond the gates of Waverley in ten minutes, I will do it. Go! I wish never to see you again."

"Go! I wish never to see you again"

Virginia whirled about, walked firmly across the lawn and entered the house. Lafe retired into the deeper shadows and stood hesitating. Suddenly he felt a light touch on his arm, and looking down, he saw Estelle.

"Don't be downhearted, Cap'n Harlan," she said, her voice showing both sympathy and fear. "I can help you. Let's go away together. Trust me, won't you, Lafe!" pleaded the girl.

For a moment he stood looking down at the girl, his face growing dark with a sudden suspicion. Then catching her roughly by the shoulder, he drew her out into a little patch of moonlight, and bending over her, muttered savagely:

"It was you, you jealous little nigger. The Squire told me you had the paper. It was you who betrayed me. I might have known better and killed yo' long ago. What's that?" In her consternation, Estelle had let fall the little bundle of trinkets and the pistol. Harlan snatched up the weapon, looked to see if it was loaded, and then shaking it before the eyes of the trembling girl, said, "I ought to put this bullet through your brain, but I must save it for bigger game. Go back to the house and keep what you have seen here to yourself. You go with me?" He laughed aloud, and tossing his black hair from his eyes, sprang down a low embankment and disappeared in the wood.

"All's well!" cried a distant sentry, and a more distant voice replied, "All's well!" But Estelle stood pale and still in the little patch of moonlight, her eyes wide, staring into the shadows.

CHAPTER XI.

THE REVELATION.

In the lamplighted coziness of the dining-room, after experiencing at supper the civilized charm of silver and white napery, Von Benzinger had left the ladies. His headquarters were established by Captain Geary in the library and the bedroom behind it. The headquarters' guard set up their tents near the stables, and sentries were posted about the house. Von Benzinger's servants were quartered with the guard. The General went to his room, wrote out a telegram, and unbuttoning his blouse, placed the paper carefully in his shirt pocket. Then he called for his horse, and telling Geary that he was going to inspect the outposts, rode away unattended. Through the window Virginia had seen him riding off in the weird night. The uncanny redness of earth and sky somehow harmonized with her impression of a mystery about this man, from whom she had received a vague impression of fear, even before Willis told her that he suspected Hamilton of treachery. How should Von Benzinger know?

After the revelation of Harlan's treachery to the South, and the certainty that somewhere that day there had been treachery to the North, Virginia was bewildered by the mazes of dishonor that were opening about her. She trusted Earl—yes; if he intended to fight for the South he would do it openly. And yet it looked so plausible. He had hired the pilots; the pilots had played false. Was the suspicion of Hamilton widespread, or was it merely Von Benzinger who suspected him? And did Von Benzinger have some motive of his own for starting the rumor? Much as she disliked the task, Virginia determined, for Earl's sake, to get all the information she possibly could out of the General.

Mrs. Poynter and the Squire had walked down toward the bay; Willis was writing in the small tower room upstairs; Geary had ridden down to Newport News, and she had sent Harlan away. The coast seemed clear for a confidential talk with Von Benzinger. He at least must be confidential, and she must seem so. She called a servant to light up the chandelier full of candles in the parlor. Idly she picked up a small book of verses by Richard Lovelace—the cloaked and rapiered cavalier who was more gentleman than poet—more soldier than gentleman, and yet, for some dozen stanzas, a peerless poet. And Virginia read with new sense of their meaning the three stanzas to Celia:

> Tell me not, sweet, I am unkind,
>   That from the nunnery
> Of thy chaste breast and quiet mind
>   To war and arms I fly.
>
> True, a new mistress now I chase—
>   The first foe in the field—
> And with a stronger faith embrace
>   A sword, a horse, a shield.
>
> But this inconstancy is such
>   As you, too, shall adore;
> I could not love thee, dear, so much
>   Loved I not honor more.

"Loved I not honor more," she mused. "Could any man ever say that more truly than Earl? He cannot be a traitor?"

Through the open window she heard the trot of hoofs on the shell road, and the challenge of the sentry. Presently Von Benzinger came in and paused in the hall.

"Ah, Miss Eggleston," he said. "I was afraid I would not see you again tonight. Do you know how rich the moonlight is upon the blossoms? Will you not watch it with me?"

"Gladly, General," said Virginia, rising and

going out with him upon the gallery. There was a light stir in the shrubbery close to the steps, but neither Virginia nor Von Benzinger observed it. The deep moonlight nearly obliterated the red tinge thrown by the burning ship; trees and bushes cast long black shadows across the lawn. Here and there in a shadow high up the light from the ship had play. The air was fragrant with the scent of crabapple and magnolia blossoms. Now and then a slow, white cloud would pass beneath the moon, darkening the world; occasionally a traveling breeze would come from afar and stir the leaves and die away in the night.

"Your work is done then for today?" Virginia said.

"For today, yes." He smiled as though the idea of his day's work pleased him. "Are you not very loyal to the South, Miss Eggleston?" he said, after a pause.

"Do you expect me to say no to that? I cannot, for I do love my country."

"Could you be friends, then, with a man who was your country's enemy?" That morning she had told him she could not. But now there rose in her mind the thought of the noon hour when, in hearing of the roar of battle, she had given her whole heart to a sailor in the Northern navy—the sailor she was trying now to save. "I did not think so till today," she said.

Von Benzinger thrilled, thinking, of course, that *he* had changed her mind.

"And today?" he said.

"Today I found that I could be friends with a man who fights as his conscience makes him— against the South."

"But suppose that, after all, this man was really fighting for the South? Could you not like him more?" Von Benzinger bent forward eagerly.

Was this a trap? Did this Federal know of Hamilton's connection with her? Did Von Benzinger suspect her of making Earl disloyal to the North? She was dazed by the quick, dangerous question, and did not reply.

"Suppose this man," he went on, "had done the South a great service—that through him the cause you love should triumph in this war? Would not that help him in your eyes?"

"If his service were done honorably—yes."

"Who can decide for another what is honorable?" he said. "The world has one pot of pitch and another of Chinese white, and it daubs with one or the other all men, and all actions. Genius works by its own laws—it brushes away conventions like to spider webs." He spoke with strange earnestness, his accent and idiom becoming slightly more foreign.

"I do not understand," she said.

"I mean that a strong man who has one great idea—one splendid purpose—should tear down what will stop him—he is not bound by common right and wrong—he is above them."

"A man should be true to his word and to his country," said Virginia, simply. She could not see what Von Benzinger's talk had to do with anything in the situation.

"Miss Eggleston," he said, "I am a lonely man. I have no one to share my triumphs—no one to tell my temptations—no one I can show the real reasons—the true motives—which justify and make honorable the things which on the surface do not look so." He moved closer to her, and his voice found strangely soft modulations. "Now, in the beauty of your Southern night, while the cannon of the ships do sleep, I would give my whole soul to you, confide all to you—and so would win your confidence, your sympathy."

"Remember, my sympathy is Confederate," she warned him. She wanted him to tell her about Hamilton, and he seemed bent on telling her about himself. She did not want his confidences—except as to one thing. It was a new experience to Virginia. She was only half aware of the power a girl like herself had over men, and she did not know how to use the power. Mrs. Poynter's skill would have spared her the necessity of listening to what she did not want to hear.

"Yes, you are Confederate," he said, "and therefore you rejoice to see that sight." He pointed toward the burning Congress. "Do you know what that is?" he went on, springing up and speaking in a low, intense voice. "That is the funeral torch of all the wooden navies of the world. That means that my thought—my iron thought—the Merrimac —is triumphant over the strongest frigates of the North. Tomorrow there will be no fleet in Hampton Roads. No Northern ship will block the way from Richmond to the sea. The Peninsular campaign, which would have poured McClellan's army through these fields, cannot be made. The Merrimac cuts off that army's base. And when the Merrimac lays Washington in ashes, your country will be recognized by all the world!"

"Splendid!" cried Virginia, swept away for an instant by the glowing image of Confederate success. "But how can you exult in the defeat of your country?"

"My country? Mon Dieu! How unjust! What are the United States to me? I have no drop of

Yankee blood. My father was an Alsatian noble, my mother a sweet peasant in the north of Spain. I was brought up in luxury, then cast penniless upon the world, without friends, influence, name. My father would have recognized me, but could not by law. I fought my way by my own will—I slaved in mine and mill and ship and camp—I learned the sciences, the tongues—I fought the world—its law, its prejudice; I made it bow to me and my idea, which was born of the anguish of my life. I came to this country a famous man. Their eyes are bounded by their shores—they do not know what I have done—they laugh at me! To-night they do not laugh!" His black-bearded lips curled open, showing his white teeth. "I come here neutral—a foreigner. The North reject me and my plans. The South was wiser—they did not re-ject."

"Do you mean that you yourself gave our government the plans to make the Merrimac?" asked Virginia, dazed, and more than half expecting an indignant denial.

Von Benzinger swept on in the intoxication of laying bare his heart to this woman who had fasci-nated him.

"To you, your Government—the Naval Secretary, Mallory, I gave the plans to make from that old wooden ship this iron Merrimac. When she—my dragon—sweeps the sea, your country will reward me with such power as I deserve."

The mask had fallen—this was the man himself. The reality overwhelmed her. What duplicity, what cunning, what blunted sense of honor! What skill to do this thing and have no soul suspect! And now in telling her, what folly, what infatuation, what weak yielding to the glamour of theatrical effect! She could not realize or grasp the thing—it dizzied her. She could not believe it; she could not believe that he was telling it, even were it true. She did not allow for the fact that he was drunk with victory, that he had just received, in the woods beyond his outposts, a telegram from Mallory, who hailed him as the savior of the South. Nor did she realize that his quick passions had made the winning of her his chief object for the moment. She felt, though, that he was trying to fascinate her by flashing himself upon her imagination as the instrument by which the South would win its independence. But he did not reckon sufficiently with her sense of honor, which was revolted by a traitor—no matter how dazzling his success, how large the scale of his schemes, or how beneficial his treachery might be to the cause she loved. He counted on her love for the South. He had no reason to suspect the counteracting love she felt for a Northern naval officer. Virginia was terrified at the vastness of his revelation. Instead of the cool, self-controlled soldier of the morning, she saw him now ablaze with passions. She had, without realizing it, unchained a terrible force. Could she control it?

"Why are you silent?" he demanded.

"I—it is so hard for me to realize—I cannot get used to your being really a Confederate. The thing is so vast—it dizzies me to think of.it."

"Ah! You see how vast it is!" he exclaimed, flattered by the word. "I was right, you have the soul to respond to a great thing. Yes, tomorrow in Richmond I will be the hero of the hour. But here tonight, I swear to you, beautiful woman, that I would rather have your gratitude, your love, than all the honors and rewards your countrymen can shower upon me."

"Do not say that," she exclaimed, desperately trying to avoid the declaration toward which he was surging.

But he swept on like a savage chief, chanting the story of his prowess—the enemies he has slain—the insults he has heaped upon their lifeless bodies. Before he cast himself and his achievements at her feet, he meant that she should realize their magnitude. "It is I who will make free your land. It is

I—here in my obscurity, neglected by the North— it is my brain which made the Merrimac. It is through me the secrets of the North are known in Richmond—it is I who ran the ships upon the shoals—my brain, moving the hands of pilots in the bay. It is I who made that crimson cloud on Hampton Roads—that fiery dawn of a new nation's day—your nation—the Confederate States of America!"

As Von Benzinger pronounced the name of the Confederacy, there was a flare of light so powerful that it quenched the moonlight. The whole landscape sprang vividly out of the night—the outline of every leaf sharp-cut. Von Benzinger and Virginia turned toward the bay. From the spot where the Congress had been burning, a cascade of fire was rushing into the sky and spreading out like a huge fan. The sound of a deep explosion filled their ears and shook the ground. From the fan burst a down-pouring rain of fire; huge blocks of flame fell back into the water and were dark.

"The Confederate States of America!" mused Virginia. "God grant that this is not a presage of their fate!"

"Bah!" said Von Benzinger. "That was the magazine of the Congress. Tomorrow we shall have some more such pretty fireworks. The Minnesota will be the first to follow her to heaven."

The sentries, violating orders, stopped at the juncture of their posts and exchanged low comments on the explosion. From the negro quarters came the high voice of a dusky parson praying for his flock in what he supposed to be the end of the world. The battle, the livid light burning through the evening, the explosion, and the great cross of fire which they had seen in the sky, had brought the black folks to the highest point of religious terror.

Willis, getting up his story of the Merrimac fight, heard the explosion, stuck his head out of the tower window, watched the geyser of fire sink back into the sea, and returning to work, gave the explosion its proper literary place in his manuscript.

The diversion had come providentially for Virginia. General von Benzinger had reached a point where he was not easy to manage. The next moment he would have asked her to become his bride in Richmond ; she would have refused him, and all hope of finding out if he meant to direct suspicion against Hamilton would have disappeared. Now she took the reins in her own hands. She began to comprehend Von Benzinger.

"But, General—to come back to what you were

telling me—how have you managed it that the Federals have not suspected your connection with the Merrimac?"

"Why should they suspect, dear lady? Nothing has been seen. Besides they have no genius for intrigue." Indeed, Von Benzinger's feline instinct for the indirect, the cunning, the subtle, had stood him in good stead. An American officer, placed as he was, would have resigned his commission, gone straight to Richmond, and tried his fortune with the Confederade Navy Department. But Von Benzinger feared that the South would be as blind as the North to the utility of the armor-plating adopted by France and England. So, still holding his commission, he sounded the Confederate Government. When Mallory and his advisors jumped at the chance to secure from the constructor of La Gloire, plans for an armored vessel which should counterbalance the immense naval preponderance of the North, Von Benzinger, for very love of it, continued to play the double game he had begun. It required skill, and he had it.

"But now," went on Virginia, closing in upon the information she was after, "they are sure the Union pilots were secretly Confederates. Will they not trace this back to you? They say some Federal officer is behind it."

"How did you know that?" asked Von Benzinger.

"Everyone—all the soldiers are talking about it."

"Do they name the officer?" asked he, his voice returning to his decisive, purposeful tones.

"It was not you," she said.

He made a gesture showing the impossibility of that.

"I think they said it was some officer of the fleet," she suggested.

"Naturally," replied he, coolly. "How should a man ashore have anything to do with it?" A pleasanter thought seemed to cross his mind, banishing the subject of his possible detection.

"What do I care, Mademoiselle Virginia," he said,—"tomorrow night in Richmond, what do I care? The Yankees can think what they will. But you—"

"But, General," she interrupted, seeing whither he was turning, "suppose the Minnesota beats the Merrimac, and the Yankees are not driven out of Hampton Roads?"

"Impossible!" he answered.

"But if?"

"There is no 'if.' The Yankees must be driven from the Roads—yes, from the sea. The Ericsson battery, the only iron ship the Union has, will be kept in the Potomac by the cowards at Washington.

And what could such a toy do with the Merrimac? The Merrimac would crush even La Gloire with her beak—she would, if that beak were, according to my specifications, steel. La Gloire would shoot at her and her shots would glance in the air."

"But if anything should happen—if the Merrimac should be blown up, for instance—you would still receive these great rewards from the Confederacy?"

"In that case, no," he smiled. "Are you afraid the Merrimac will be blown up?"

"It would surely be a great misfortune for the South," she said, sincerely. "But in such a case, would you not fear the Federals would find out your—" she checked the word "treachery" upon her lips—"find out what you have done for us?"

"You look far ahead," he said, wondering why she pressed the point so.

"It is but my solicitude."

So it was, oh deceitful Virginia, intriguing against an arch-intriguer, deceiving a past-master of deceit. It was solicitude for Hamilton down yonder in the bay, whose ship was doomed to sink or burn tomorrow, whose life and honor, as she now saw well, would be sacrificed by this powerful, unscrupulous man, if it became necessary to shield himself.

Virginia had found out what she wanted to know

and far more.   And in allaying his suspicion she did more than she meant.   Her sweet speech—its irony quite unperceived by him—sent through Von Benzinger a delicious thrill that brought him to his knees with words of burning love upon his lips. Fortunately a horseman, riding fast, pulled up at the gate just then and was passed by the sentry. Von Benzinger, glowing with delighted hope, did not hear or see.

"Someone is coming, General," she said.

"Exasperating!" he exclaimed.   It was very awkward to rise from one's knees under such circumstances.   But to him, already possessed with the idea that he had made a deep impression upon her heart, her words seemed to indicate that when the opportunity came she would listen gladly to his words of love.

The rider was Captain Geary.   Instead of taking his horse to the stable or calling a man, he tied the animal in front of the house, and started rapidly up the steps.   Catching sight of Von Benzinger's white hair upon the veranda, he saluted and said:

"General, I have news of the utmost importance." Geary did not see Virginia sitting in the shadow of the veranda roof.   Acknowledging the salute, Von Benzinger stepped toward the Captain.   He did not care what Virginia heard, for she would soon be his.

"Well?" said he, expectantly.

"The Monitor—Ericsson's new floating battery —has come into the Roads from New York, and will remain here tomorrow to fight the Merrimac." Geary's voice was low and earnest.

"The Monitor!" exclaimed Von Benzinger, with astonishment. "The Monitor was ordered from New York to Washington."

"Her commander, Lieutenant Worden, will disobey orders, and remain here tomorrow. He believes the Monitor can whip the Merrimac and save the fleet."

"Diable!" said Von Benzinger, under his breath. And then to account for his displeasure, he said, quickly: "The Monitor will be destroyed. Worden should obey orders."

"Certainly, sir, but he won't do it. And what is more, this Lieutenant Hamilton, whom you suspect of treachery, is to pilot the Monitor in the battle. When I heard it, I hastened to you, that you might stop him."

"I will stop him," said Von Benzinger, savagely.

There was a quick movement on the veranda. "Who's that?" asked Geary, startled.

"You are right, Geary," said Von Benzinger,

standing so the light from the hall fell into the Captain's eyes. "This is very important."

Pretending to be pondering the news, the General paid no attention to Geary's startled question. He did not care to let his adjutant know that he had permitted Federal secrets to be discussed in Virginia's hearing. "Take your horse around, and come to my room." Before the Captain's return, Virginia could slip quietly into the house. As he went down the steps, Geary peered blinkingly into the gallery, but could see nothing.

CHAPTER XII.

SHUT IN.

Geary out of the way for the moment, Von Benzinger stepped quickly to Virginia, and said: "The Captain must not know you were here. Good-night, sweet one. My secret, like my heart, is yours, yours only. Guard it well. I trust you." He pressed her hands. They were like ice. "Are you ill?" he asked.

She could hardly speak for the terror that had sprung up in her. "Today has been too much—the battle—the anxiety—good-night." She could not force herself to give him her hand. She fled into the house and up to her room. She must think. She must act. Act quickly. She was alone. If only Cora were here—ah, what could Cora do against Von Benzinger? She must accuse Von Benzinger. Then at the thought she laughed hysterically. Who would believe her?—the story was so wild, so impossible. And coming from her—a Southerner—

to shield Hamilton, the Southerner, who was accused of treason to the North! Her story would confirm his guilt. What power guarded this man Von Benzinger and made him like his Merrimac—invulnerable?

"What shall I do, what can be done?" Ah, there was one thing. She could forewarn Earl of the impending accusation. He might take steps to meet it. Seth knew the way to him—she must send Seth.

She could see the square of light cast from the tower window upon the foliage of the elm outside. A shadow passed across the square. It was Willis—quiet, determined Willis, Earl's friend, who had asked her help for Earl. She flew to his door and knocked. "Mr. Willis," she called, in a low voice, "Mr. Willis!" Willis threw open the door and the light fell upon her pale face and into her wild eyes.

"Good heavens, Miss Eggleston, what has happened?" he asked.

"Will you believe me, Mr. Willis? Will you believe I am telling you the truth? I swear it is the truth."

"Easy, easy," said Willis, getting possession of himself. "Now, take it easy, Miss Eggleston, and tell me quietly. I'll believe you quicker than Holy Writ, whatever you may say."

"General von Benzinger is a Confederate. He designed the Merrimac."

Willis started. Then he stared. "Will you please say that again?" he said, slowly.

"I knew you'd not believe me!" she cried, in despair.

"Hold on," he said. "Von Benzinger—the Merrimac. By Jimtown!"

"Oh, please believe me, Mr. Willis. Earl's life and honor are at stake."

"Von Benzinger—the Merrimac. Why, what a cussed fool I've been. It's plain as print. La Gloire is French for Merrimac. I'm poor at French. Well, Miss Eggleston, what next?—speak low."

"The Monitor has come—to fight the Merrimac. Oh—what if I lose the battle by doing this?" A sudden pang of loyalty revealed to her that to save Hamilton she must work against the South—the Merrimac—Von Benzinger. But Earl—his honor —dearer to him than life. "Oh!" she cried, "it cannot be disloyal to save the true man from the false —the noble enemy from the treacherous friend."

"Disloyal?" said Willis. "Maybe it's disloyal, Miss Eggleston, but it's right, and you know it. What about the Monitor?"

"Earl is to pilot her. Von Benzinger will accuse him to stop him—so the Merrimac can win. Go down and warn him, Mr. Willis. Take Bay Nellie, and go quickly or it may be too late."

"Good thing enough to warn him," said Willis, "but that ain't enough. Can't you send someone else? I'd like to stay here and watch things. We ought to get hold of something on Von Benzinger. It's not easy—the old fox. And the story is so impossible, he's safe. *I* believe it," he hastened to say, "I believe anything about that man—but other people won't. Let me see?" He folded his arms and knitted his brows, thinking. From the gallery steps came the sound of Von Benzinger's voice, talking excitedly. "Now what's that?" said Willis. "I believe that's worth hearing."

The correspondent slipped softly down the back way, leaving Virginia alone.

She must send Seth then, after all. Willis could do more good here. She went to her room, wrote rapidly a note of warning to Earl. Then she went to Seth's room in the back of the house, woke him, told him he must dress himself, saddle a horse and ride to the bay. He was to come to her room for the note and his instructions. Virginia slipped back to her room and waited in an agony of suspense. How slow Seth was! What was Willis doing? If the note were only safely started! The time was interminable, and she had a feeling that things were happening beneath her in the yard. She thought she heard the voice of Harlan. Surely it could not be. Seth came at last and took the note. She could see that her manner terrified him. "Go quietly," she said, "and saddle the horse. The countersign is 'Virginia, Fair, Rebel.' You say the first word, the sentry the second, and you the third."

"I done hear 'em do it, Miss Virginia. I knows how. Don' yo' worry, Miss Virginia, I take yo' note to de ship, even if I is scared. I do it fo' yo'."

"Don't stop; don't stop to talk, but go." Seth left for the stable, and again came that dreadful fear of unknown things happening about her. She thought she saw figures moving in the shadows.

"Halt!" rang the sentry's voice in the still night. The cold, sharp word gave Virginia a violent start. Who was leaving?—it was not time for Seth. There was a moment's pause while the countersign was given.

"The countersign is right—pass on."

Two minutes later came again that startling "Halt!" Again someone was passed.

Silence again. Then she heard someone speaking low to the sentry. Then the speaker entered the house. A moment later she heard Von Benzinger come in, and then his voice, down stairs. She slipped to the banister and listened. "Captain

Geary," said the General, "I have instructed the sentries to pass no one whatever, with or without the countersign. There are spies here. You will so inform the officer of the guard."

A great sickening fear came over Virginia and she leaned back against the wall. Whom did he mean? Could it be Harlan? No. What had happened? Where was Willis? Was he accused? Seth could not get through with his message.

She heard Geary's footsteps. He was going to give the order to the guard.

"And, Geary," came the General's voice again—bitter, confident. "Instruct the guard to arrest and search all those who try to pass." If Seth reached the sentry before she could stop him, her note warning Hamilton against the accusation would soon be in Von Benzinger's hands.

CHAPTER XIII.

THE FATAL SHOT.

When Virginia left Von Benzinger on the gallery, he turned his mind to the new factor in his problem—the Monitor. Others thought her an ingenious toy; he knew she was dangerous. The Merrimac could have destroyed the wooden fleet without the co-operation of the Union pilots. They had simply made assurance doubly sure. Now it was to be iron against iron, and the Monitor's pilot might decide the battle. If he could remove Hamilton, there would be absolutely no one in the fleet who knew the water and could be trusted. Von Benzinger had promised the Confederate Government to clear the Roads. If he failed, they owed him nothing—and, in the eyes of the world, his invention would be outclassed by Ericsson's; the world would never even hear of him as the inventor of the Merrimac. Yes, Hamilton must be accused, but, being accused, he must be convicted. If the

11

Monitor did win, Von Benzinger must remain a Federal. To do that safely, someone else had to be proved the briber of the pilots. Hamilton had hired them; he was open to suspicion, but there must be proof. Where find it? How make it? What things could be twisted into proof? Geary knew nothing more than he had told. Geary would not help him manufacture evidence. He must find someone who would. He must find someone who knew Hamilton. But, who? Willis would not do—he was too clever. These things flashed through Von Benzinger's agile mind in far less time than it takes to write them. The elements of the situation were grasped by him all at once and as a whole. Thinking, waiting for Geary, he had descended the steps, his hands behind him, his head bowed, his eyes upon the ground.

"Von Benzinger!" said a hoarse, low voice, close by. In spite of his steady nerves, the General started and whirled toward the sound of the voice. It came from the shrubbery, not ten feet from where he had revealed his secret to Virginia.

"Who's there?" he demanded, and in his voice was fear—a feeling he had almost forgotten. He felt for his pistol—it was not there. The bushes parted and a man stepped out. The General glared at him.

"I want to see you, Von Benzinger."

"Who are you?" hissed Von Benzinger.

"I was introduced to you this morning as Robertson."

"Lafe Harlan! You eavesdropper! I'll have the soldiers finish *you*!" Von Benzinger was about to call the corporal of the guard.

"Hold on," said Harlan. "I know your whole scheme. I know what'll smash you, and I know what'll save you. You can help me or smash me, Von Benzinger, but don't you believe I can't do the same to you. If I drop dead right here, your goose is cooked. I tell you, if you don't hear what I say, you're a goner."

Geary came suddenly around the house. Harlan made a quick movement toward the bushes. It was too late. Von Benzinger motioned to him to stand still.

"There's a man here, Captain," said the General, calmly, "who may have valuable information. I will examine him. You may get up that order about the battalion adjutants."

With a "yes, sir," and a glance of curiosity at Harlan, Geary went on into the house.

"Now, what do you know?" asked Von Benzinger.

"First, I know all about Hamilton," answered

Harlan, watching the effect of his words. He was not disappointed. Von Benzinger became visibly interested.

"Next, I can help you fix him. And, then, there's something else I'll tell you *after* you say what you'll do for me."

"What do you want?"

"When you join the Confeds I want you to fix 'em so they won't shoot me for this damned reward. And just now, I want a paper that'll take me through any bluecoat guard line."

"I'll give you a pass if your information's worth it."

"Then will you promise to help me with the Confeds? I'll help you now, if you will." Harlan spoke pleadingly, and took hold of the General's arm.

"Humph!" Von Benzinger brushed his sleeve. "You help me!" he said, contemptuously. "I plan a thing and do it against hell. You bend either way to any pressure. Just understand the difference."

"The difference is, I'm found out and you ain't— yet," said Harlan.

"Fools are found out, not men of sense."

"Men of sense don't tell their secrets to women whose lovers are at stake."

"Except when women do not love their lovers," retorted Von Benzinger, scornfully. "She will not betray me for your sake, eavesdropper."

"You fool, she loves Lieutenant Hamilton!"

"What!" exclaimed Von Benzinger.

"She will betray you to save Hamilton."

"Impossible!"

"Don't I know?" broke out Harlan, with vehemence, "hasn't he stolen her from me—wasn't he here this morning makin' love to her? Didn't she drive me away like a dog? Didn't she make you tell her all you knew, so's to tell him? I saw through her game, but you didn't—oh, no! I'll bet she's sending word to him this minute."

Von Benzinger was stunned. For a moment he was silent, contemplating his colossal folly. "Hamilton!" he groaned. "Hamilton! And I told her— oh, fool, fool, fool! Caught with poisoned honey! Fooled like a boy of twenty by a woman's lies! And she—the snake!" He became speechless with rage. Never had his tremendous egotism received such a blow, never had he been so duped, and duped with so little effort. She had simply let him talk, let him take things for granted. He had been quick to love her, if love it could be called. Now he hated her with all the force of his volcanic nature. His paroxysm of anger passed, he became quiet, got control of his mind, and then he became dangerous.

"I will crush her," he said. And truly, though Virginia had so easily outwitted him so far, the young girl had no more chance against Von Benzinger than the Cumberland had against the Merrimac. "But first for Monsieur Hamilton," said the General. "You would like to see him hang?"

"Would I?" asked Harlan, in a tone that left no doubt about it.

Slipping from bush to bush, nearer and nearer, came Willis, until he could hear comfortably all that passed between the two men.

"What proof is there, then, that the brave Monsieur Hamilton bribed the pilots?"

"Didn't he hire 'em three months ago? Ain't he a Southerner? Ain't he in love with a red-hot rebel?"

"Presumptions, not proofs," said Von Benzinger. "Did you betray Confederate secrets to Federals?"

"What if I did?"

"Look, Mr. Harlan. You come to me from the Confederate lines. You are really a Union spy. You say to me that Buchanan has a letter from Hamilton in which the Lieutenant promises to bribe the pilots. You have seen this letter. Do you understand?"

"Yes," said Harlan, admiringly.

"I vouch for your past services, send you to General Wool, who hears your story, and informs Captain Marston, the senior naval officer."

"Yes," said Harlan.

"Hamilton is arrested on the strength of your story and my endorsement of your character."

"Yes."

"You will do this?"

"I will," said Harlan.

"Can you get from the fort to the Merrimac?"

"Yes, but the sailors may have seen the papers lately. They'd turn me over for the reward."

"Not when you carry a cipher dispatch to the ship's captain."

"Will you give me one?"

"Yes. In two parts. Part one will contain tactical hints for Buchanan concerning the Monitor. Part two will be such a note as Buchanan might write to Hamilton about the pilots. I will ask Buchanan to copy in his handwriting this note and give it to.you. Do you understand?"

"Not quite," said Harlan.

"Wool has letters in Buchanan's handwriting," explained Von Benzinger, patiently. "Now, you will have this note from Buchanan to Hamilton, dated, say, a week ago, and proving that Hamilton had agreed to bribe the pilots. You go back to General Wool, give him this note, and soon afterward the happy lover of Miss Eggleston will decorate the yard arm of his ship."

"I see," said Harlan, enthusiastically. "You certainly have got brains, General."

"Could you go to the Merrimac first and still reach the fort by daylight?"

"What time is it now?"

"After ten."

"Let's see—two—nine—sixteen miles. Easy."

"Then do it. The cipher to Buchanan, on the Merrimac—my message and Buchanan's note to Wool, at the fort. Is it clear?"

"Clear as a bell," answered Harlan.

"It is a simple plan. A coward could not carry it out, but, stupid as you are, you are no coward. If all succeeds, you can safely go with me to Richmond. Remember, if I fall, you fall. Your fate is linked with mine. Wait here. I will write the cipher and the note to Wool." Von Benzinger went up the steps and into the house. He went to his room, sat down and wrote:

HEADQUARTERS SECOND BRIGADE, FIRST DIVISION,
DEPARTMENT OF VIRGINIA,
WAVERLEY, VA., March 8, 1862.

To MAJOR GENERAL WOOL,

Commanding Department of Virginia, Fort Monroe:

Sir:—I strongly suspect the Virginian, Lieutenant Earl Hamilton, U. S. N., now on the Minnesota, of being in communication with Richmond and of inducing pilots to ground ships. The bearer of this note has strong confirmation, which he will lay before you. He has already rendered important secret service. Virginia Eggleston, of Waverley plantation, is probably Hamilton's accomplice. Am watching her. Please inform Captain Marston.

Respectfully, your obedient servant,

HUGO VON BENZINGER,

Brigadier-General, Commanding.

In cipher, he wrote:—

FLAG OFFICER FRANKLIN BUCHANAN,

Commanding Merrimac.

Monitor in Roads and will fight you tomorrow. Board her, lash her, cover turrets with tarpaulins, throw in hand-grenades.   VON B.

Give to bearer a copy, in your handwriting, of the following note:

March 3, 1862.

LIEUTENANT E. H.,

On Minnesota.

Your proposal concerning pilots is approved. Will count on you. Merrimac will attack on seventh or eighth.

FRANKLIN BUCHANAN, C. S. N.

The note from Buchanan to Hamilton was written, not in cipher, but in a disguised hand. If it fell, accidentally, into Federal hands, it would convict, not Von Benzinger, but Hamilton.

As Von Benzinger finished writing the dispatches, his eye fell on his pistol. Having just felt the need of it, and realizing that he was playing a desperate game that night, he put it on.

Willis, lying in the shrubbery, also felt the need of a pistol, and remembered the two he had seen lying in their case on the mantel in the dining-room. He moved away, as he had come, unseen by Harlan. Passing around the house, he stepped through the dining-room window, and, feeling in the dark, found one of the ivory-mounted pistols still lying in its case. The other was gone. He stepped to the light of the window, found the pistol loaded, and put it carefully into his pocket. "The key to this situation," he reflected, "is Von Benzinger's cipher to the Merrimac. I must have it. I wonder if it's written yet." Dangerous as it would be, he determined to go to Von Benzinger at his desk, cover him with his pistol, and demand the cipher. He tiptoed through the dark dining-room, opened the door slightly, and looked across the hall to Von Benzinger's room. The light was still burning, but the General had finished writing and was gone. "He's practiced that cipher," thought Willis, "I wonder if it's a hard one to read when you already know what's in it? But, first catch your cipher." He stepped through the window, and heard the sentry's startling "Halt!" "That's Harlan going out," he thought. Behind the house he saw Seth slipping off toward the stable. Willis walked to the front of the house, approached the gate, was challenged and passed. Immediately afterward Von Benzinger came from the house and said something to the sentry. Willis was just in time to avoid being caught in the trap of the guard-line. Being through it, he walked briskly down the road to Newport—after Harlan.

It was then that Virginia, tortured with terrible surmises, heard Von Benzinger repeat to Geary his order to the guard—an order which made prisoner every soul of the Waverley household. The fatal words, "arrest and search all those who try to pass," were yet ringing in her ears, when, through the open window of her room, she heard Seth's horse trot past the house. He must not reach the sentry at the gate. Down the stairs she darted, trying to make no noise which would attract and draw after her the dreadful man whose web was closing round her. Through the door she sped, and into the night.

"Seth, Seth!" she called, but Seth was already so near the sentry that she dared not call out loud, and her voice was drowned in the sound of horse's hoofs. The terrible "Halt!" rang out; the poor old darky stumbled pitifully through his well-rehearsed countersign—in vain. He was ruthlessly pulled from his horse; the sentry called the corporal of the guard; the corporal came. He found and roughly took the precious note, and led old Seth away—whimpering—pleading to ears that were deaf to all but "orders." Virginia did not plead nor stir. She knew too well how vain it was, how impossible to sway these men from duty. She realized, as the corporal took the note, that no power or act or word of hers could keep it from Von Benzinger. However much he already knew, he would soon know all—he would know she was his bitterest enemy—alone—a prisoner—in his power. Utter despair for her own fate overpowered her. The one hope was that Willis had got through the lines and would do something to save Earl. The corporal had taken Seth to the guard tent, near the stable; the sentry at the gate walked up and down his post outside the wall. Desolate, helpless, Virginia stood outside her house, within the walls of which a powerful enemy was plotting her destruction. Why didn't Cora come back? Would the sentry let her in?

From the direction of the road to Newport, startling Virginia's shaken nerves, rang out two pistol shots in quick succession. What did they mean —those shots? She waited, listening. The sentry stopped. No sound—nothing. Yes, there was a man running—running this way—running heavily. In her anxiety to see who it was, Virginia, forgetting herself and her fear lest Von Benzinger should see her, took a step toward the gate. The light from the hall lamp fell full upon her. The runner neared the gate.

"Halt!" cried the sentry, but the man kept on. He ran like a man in his sleep—fleeing from some unknown terror. The swing of his elbows turned his whole body from side to side.

"Halt, or I fire!" shouted the sentry.

Past the sentry, through the gate, straight up the path toward her, came the man with that terrible, automatic trot. The sentry leveled his musket, but did not fire, for fear of striking the girl. Virginia stood fascinated. The light fell on the man's white face—the eyes fixed and staring—blood pouring from his mouth. She heard someone behind her, but could not turn. Was this vision real, or a dream? She heard a pistol shot, the horrid, running Thing lurched forward and fell in the gravel, clutching sightlessly at her skirt. She saw her pistol in its hand, she saw the hand relax and the pistol fall at her feet. She saw Von Benzinger stoop over the fallen man and turn him on his back. The man groaned, his rigid limbs relaxed. Horrible! It was Lafe Harlan. Estelle came from somewhere, and with one wild look knelt beside the man she loved, wiping the blood from his mouth. Von Benzinger pushed her aside and felt in Harlan's pockets.

"Where are those dispatches?" he demanded. Others were looking on, now—Virginia did not know who they were. "Who has done this? Who shot you?" went on Von Benzinger, shaking the body. The man fought for breath, his body stiffened again, through the gurgle in his throat came the one word, "Virginia!" The body relaxed in death—there was an instant of unbroken silence— the eyes of the group about Virginia turned in consternation from the dead man to her.

General von Benzinger rose from his position beside the body. His eyes fell on Virginia's pistol lying at her feet. He picked it up, looked at it, drew himself up.

"Virginia Eggleston," he said, "you will be tried by courtmartial as a Confederate spy, and for the murder of the Union messenger—Lafe Harlan!"

" Virginia Eggleston," he said, " you will be tried by courtmartial as a
Confederate spy."

CHAPTER XIV.

THE COURTMARTIAL.

Lafe Harlan was dead. Major Cuthbertson, the brigade surgeon, had said so, officially. When he had finished his report, he laid before General von Benzinger, together with the pistol found at Virginia's feet, a small package sealed with red sealing wax. Across the face of this package was written, "Bullet taken from the body of Lafe Harlan," together with the name of the surgeon. Captain Geary and Lieutenant Edwards had endorsed it as witnesses.

"Does this bullet fit the pistol?" inquired the General, a bright spot burning in each cheek, despite his masterful effort to appear unconcerned.

"Exactly," replied the surgeon. "The pistol is of a foreign make, and bullets to fit it must be run in a peculiar mould. The owner of the weapon should have such an instrument."

"Have you said as much in your report?"

"Yes."

"The moulds might be something after the fashion of these, I suppose?" said the General, withdrawing from a paper a small pair of steel bullet moulds, exquisitely wrought, and handing them to the surgeon.

"The bullet was run in this mould," said the surgeon, after a moment's examination. "I am sure of it. The caliber is an odd one, as you can see, and this small thread running about the center is clearly marked in the bullet I have placed in evidence."

"Thank you," said General von Benzinger, placing the moulds by the side of the pistol. "You will find cigars in the adjoining room. I will see you there presently."

When he was again alone, General von Benzinger took up a pen, and, bending over the table, began writing slowly and with great care, seeming to weigh each word before committing it to paper. He was compiling the charges, and his fate depended, in a great measure, on the impression those charges should make. It was necessary that they should be completed at once, so that the findings might reach General Wool in time to have Hamilton taken from the Monitor before her duel with the Merrimac—the duel sure to begin with the morning. The summons for officers to sit on the courtmartial had already been prepared, and Edwards was ordered to have them served with all possible dispatch.

Out in the yard, at the orderlies' quarters, there were hurried preparations and mounting in hot haste, not without much grumbling and many good, round oaths by the men at having to do extra duty. Half an hour later, orderlies were spurring about among the tents of the camps on the plain below, stumbling over invisible tent ropes, and answering challenges that came with startling suddenness from shadowy places. When the officer for whom one of them was searching was finally found, he sat up on his blanket, rubbed his eyes, and demanded, "What it was all about?" But when he had received the document the orderly presented, and read it, either in the moonlight or by the faint gleam of a tallow held dangerously near his nose by his yawning "striker," he hurriedly returned his compliments to the General, with the information that he would report at once. Then he dressed himself with as much care and dignity as a crowded tent and a limited field equipment allowed. Afterward, he trotted away toward Waverley, his orderly, with more or less jerking of reins and spurring of heels, holding his proper distance in the rear.

While these hurried preparations for the trial were going forward, Estelle sat in a dark corner of one of the whitewashed negro cabins, clutching her knees with her hands, shivering, moaning and muttering self-reproaches, unintelligible to the slaves standing silently about, who attributed her startled looks and broken sentences to grief for her young mistress. They were ignorant of the part she had contributed to the tragedy. Had they known, they would not have understood. She did not understand it all herself. It was like some awful nightmare in which she struggled, but from which she could not awake. From the moment Harlan had left her in the woods, his mocking laugh ringing in her ears, until she knelt beside his bleeding body upon the lawn at Waverley, time was a blank to her. There she had heard Virginia accused of his murder, and seen her led away, but, even to her dulled perceptions, her mistress seemed an angel about whom the garment of innocence fell like a mantle of light. Cowering there on the ground, she had seen the big surgeon stride into the yard, bend over the body of the fallen man, place his hand over his heart, lift the lids from the dull, staring eyes, and say—"the man is dead." A new horror seized her at the words, and, springing up, she had fled to the negro quarters, and, going in at the first open door, had crouched there like a hunted animal wounded to the death.

The other slaves were almost as wild with grief as Estelle. Everywhere there was wailing and tears, for Virginia was to them a spirit of goodness, and the awful charge against her seemed to these superstitious creatures the work of some demon whose power was not to be overcome by anything less than the supernatural. Not one of these simple, timid folk but would have gone to any lengths to have saved their young mistress one pang of pain, but against this hidden "Spirit of Evil" they dared not even complain. And so they drew close together in their cabins, moaning and wringing their hands—helpless and afraid.

Up on the hill, in the big dining-room that had been prepared for the courtmartial, the officers were already beginning to gather. A captain and two lieutenants, forming a group near the window that opened on the gallery, conversed about the tragedy in low tones. A burly man, with fierce mustache and bristling brows, who wore the insignia of a major on his shoulder straps, stood alone at the other end of the room, his back to the sideboard. In his hand he held a formidable-looking document, which he was scanning with great care. He was the Judge Advocate, who was to represent the Government. The paper he was reading contained the charges against Virginia, compiled by General von Benzinger.

Before the house, orderlies walked back and forth along the drive, each leading two horses, his own and his commander's. When they passed each other, as they often did in their travel back and forth, they exchanged comments on the strange story, expressing opinions in short, jerky sentences barren of adjectives—a diction peculiar to the rank and file of the American army. Other officers came at intervals, and the steady beat of steel-shod hoofs on the shell road seemed to strike a minor chord in the solemn stillness of the night. Along the distant shore the waves broke with a muffled sound that drifted inland like the troubled throbbings of a giant heart. And in a guarded room of the old, rambling, ivy-mantled house, Virginia sat alone, waiting to be summoned before the tribunal which held in its hand—her life.

Soon after midnight the guard entered the prisoner's room and told her she was to go with them to the courtroom. As she passed along the hall, Black Mammie, kneeling near the door of her chamber, crept forward with clasped hands and streaming eyes, begging the guards to be merciful to her mistress.

"Kill ole Brack Mammie, Marse Sojer, but don' fo' de Lawd sake hu't ma honey chile—sweetes' chile yo' ole Brack Mammie evah nussed, dat yo' is honey, de sweetes' an' de bes'! Fo' Lawd sake, Marse Sojer, don' take away ma po' honey chile."

Virginia bent down and twined her arm tenderly about the neck of the black woman.

"Don't worry, Mammie," she said. "They will not harm me. Go to bed now, and think no more about it. Everything will be right in the morning."

"Agin' orders, Miss," said one of the guards. "You're not to talk to anyone until after the trial. Sorry, Miss, but it's orders."

"I understand," said Virginia, rising, "and I'll make you as little trouble as possible. Good night, Mammie." She bent to kiss the tear-wet cheek of the nurse. "I am ready."

"Ma po' honey chile," moaned the negress, as Virginia moved away, between two heavily tramping guards. "W'y don' yo' take her ole Brack Mammie, Marse Sojer? She done ready fo' ter die, on'y don' ha'm huh, honey, Marse Sojer; don' ha'm huh Mammie's honey chile!"

"Don't Mammie!" cried Virginia, halting on the landing, and smiling bravely. "You hurt me. Go to bed and come to me early in the morning. The trouble will be over then."

"Hurry up there, men!" called a sergeant from the hall below. "They're waitin' for ye."

When Virginia entered the dining-room, the officers were seated about the table, six on each side. Two chairs, one at either end of the table, were unoccupied. As she came in, the men got up, rather awkwardly, and, removing their hats, stood until she had been conducted to the lower end of the room and was seated in a chair placed for her by a Lieutenant Harper, who was acting as recorder. A moment later the Judge Advocate came in and took a seat near Virginia, at the lower end of the table. He was followed by a small man with red, bushy hair, standing straight on his head, a straggling, close-clipped, red beard, small, piercing, brown eyes, and a quick, nervous manner. The others arose and saluted, as he took the remaining vacant chair at the head of the table. The officer nearest him addressed him as Mr. President, and spoke a few words in a low tone, glancing in the direction of Virginia. The President shook his head slowly two or three times, fired a piercing look at the prisoner, and sat down. Edwards began to straighten out the papers before him. A sallow, light-haired man came and stood by Virginia's chair, and she was told that he was to act as her attorney.

Virginia tried to keep all these things in her mind, to feel that all this precision and care meant life or death to her, but her thoughts ran away from her continually and lingered over the moonlit waters of Hampton Roads, and about the Minnesota, and the new Monitor that Earl Hamilton was to pilot tomorrow in the duel between it and that awful force—the Merrimac. Was he thinking of her? Would he come unhurt from tomorrow's struggle, as he did from that of yesterday? Then she remembered Von Benzinger's words, "he must be stopped," and a mist swam before her eyes, and a great fear took possession of her—a fear that Von Benzinger might know of her scene with Willis and have had him, too, arrested. If that were so, the blow would fall upon Hamilton without warning, and, Willis had said, a man accused of such a crime would have no chance to defend himself. She must go herself and warn him. Bay Nellie would carry her safely to the water, and then—

"Virginia Eggleston!"

The name thundered in her ears like the roar of a thousand guns. Why did the girl not answer? It was best she should do nothing to offend these men. But that was her own name. Certainly, she would stand up and answer any questions they might ask her. She was ignorant of military matters. She had never heard of a courtmartial before tonight.

"Virginia Eggleston, you are charged with plotting to destroy the Union fleet and with the murder of Lafe Harlan, a Union messenger. Are you guilty or not guilty?"

She knew that it was the Judge Advocate speaking, and that there were not two Virginias, and yet she waited and listened for the other one to reply. Why was not the answer forthcoming? There was nothing to fear, nothing to conceal, the girl was innocent. And then came the realization that somehow she must reply for this other Virginia who was on trial for her life.

"Do you refuse to answer?" How cold and level the tones of that voice. Oh, no, she did not refuse to answer. She did not hear you. I will answer for her, sir. She is not guilty. There has been a terrible mistake somewhere. General von Benzinger is guilty, but that you all know better than I can tell you; but Virginia, she is just a young girl who loves the blue skies, and the fields, the river, the slaves, Bay Nellie, and—and Hamilton. Yes, surely, she loves Lieutenant Hamilton, although she cannot tell you why, since he is fighting against her country. He is out there now preparing to guide this new monster that came suddenly out of the smoke and flame last night, to try results with that other and greater monster that had roared about the Roads all yesterday.

"Does the prisoner object to the introduction of General von Benzinger's statement of the case and the reasons which led him to make the arrest?" It was the same hard, cold voice, the same level tone, every word spoken distinctly, with a little pause after each. It sounded like the dropping of pebbles, one after another, into a wooden bowl. But the prisoner must answer. If they would be patient a moment she would urge Virginia—but, was she not herself Virginia? No, she had no objections. He could read on. If only they would not disturb her. She wished to think of the morrow, of Earl, of the time when the war would be over, and they could sit once more together on the vine-wreathed gallery at Waverley.

The dropping of the pebbles into the bowl echoed her thoughts, or, rather, mingled with them and became a part of them. Now they were telling how she had invited Hamilton to visit her in the morning, of their meeting in the garden, of her passionate appeal to him to abandon the ship, flee from the danger, and come back to the South, and loyalty, and her. Now they were repeating the words of her note to him after the battle, and his message of assurance that he was safe. Then it was the letter that she had written to warn him of Von Benzinger's charges. What would the other Virginia think of this? how would she account for it? Was Von Benzinger omnipotent, that he could thus read the secrets of the soul? The pebbles were dropping one by one, and each one was a word of her letter. "Earl. You are suspected of having bribed the pilots who ran the ships aground. General von Benzinger is sending word to General Wool, so that you may not be allowed to pilot the Monitor. I could not, even to save your life, betray secrets of the Confederacy, but Von Benzinger is a traitor. Be warned—save yourself and love—Virginia." What was strange in this letter that the men around the board should smile knowingly and nod their heads at one another? Was it so wicked to send a warning to an old friend whom a traitor was plotting to destroy? The reference to General von Benzinger seemed to strike on her ear curiously. Why should it appear to have a double meaning, even to her? Surely there was nothing of this in her mind when she wrote it. Yet the men smiled when it was read and nodded significantly.

Suddenly the story the pebbles were telling changed. They were telling of Harlan, her meetings with him, her denunciation of him, the pistol shots, his death, his dying cry of "Virginia!" Back and forth along the chain, that link by link had been woven of her acts and words, her dazed mind wandered, searching in vain for the flaw that must be there. By and by she began to wonder if the Virginia who was on trial was not, after all, guilty. How could it be otherwise? The dropping of the pebbles ceased, and someone was holding up a pistol, and asking if it were not hers, and when she had last seen it? Then the dropping continued, telling now of a surgeon, and wounds, and a bullet. The pebbles were larger now, and the bowl must soon be filled.

Then the wooden bowl became suddenly as big as half the world, and there were great waves of water dashing over the pebbles, which were boulders now. And far out on the storm-tossed sea, leagues and leagues from shore, a tiny boat was pitching and plunging here and there. There was a woman in the boat. It was the prisoner, and she was crying for help. She stretched out her arms in a vain attempt at rescue. A great wave lifted high in the air and rushed upon the boat; there was a sudden roar as if the heavens had fallen, and the waters swept over everything, and blotted out the world.

* * * * * * * *

An hour before the dawn, the officers rode down the shell road from Waverley to their respective commands. The trial was over, the evidence had been summed up, the Judge Advocate had made his cold, clear, unprejudiced statement of the facts, and the verdict had been signed and placed in the hands of General von Benzinger.

The Judge Advocate had gone, and Von Benzinger stood with the findings of the courtmartial in his hand. He turned the key in the door, and, sitting down at the table near the window, opened the document. Man of steel as he had proven himself to be, his fingers trembled and his hand shook as he unfolded the closely written sheets. All night he had not closed his eyes, and the strain was beginning to tell.

"Of the first specification, guilty," he read, and his eyes, dull with long watching, burned anew.

"Of the second specification, guilty."

"Of the third specification, guilty."

"Of the fourth specification, guilty."

"Of the fifth specification, guilty."

"Of the charge—guilty."

The red spots were burning in his cheeks like two

tiny suns. He folded the papers carefully. "It yet lacks the signature of General Wool," he whispered. He shut the fatal document in his two hands, held it down upon the table and looked at it steadily. Little by little his head dropped forward. At last his forehead rested upon the paper.

From the Confederate lines a signal rocket shot straight into the darkened sky. A wave of red light flashed across the window and lit up the room. It fell upon the sleeping man, and his white hair took on a crimson hue, as though it had been dipped in blood.

CHAPTER XV.

THE MONITOR.

Miles and miles to the northward, that Saturday afternoon, the waveworn crew of the Monitor, passing out of the storm that threatened their destruction, had heard the sound of distant cannon. Night fell, and they saw before them the "crimson cloud on Hampton Roads" which the Merrimac had made. Anchoring near the fort, they learned the details of the day's disaster. Their commander, Worden, decided that on the morrow the place for his strange, new craft was Hampton Roads, not Washington. Steaming over to the Minnesota, the Monitor dropped anchor under the frigate's lofty counter and waited for the morning and the Merrimac. No man of that crew slept that night. Since they left New York, three days before, no man had slept. They had been fighting the sea; now they repaired the damage of that fight, and prepared for battle with the deadliest vessel that ever floated.

To the onlookers, it was laughable to see this little vessel—this "cheese box on a plank"—assume the role of guardian of the towering frigate. The crew of the Minnesota had no hope that the new arrival could resist the destroyer of the Cumberland and Congress. But they admired the little fellow's pluck. The officers and men of the Monitor knew little more about their vessel's fighting qualities than the sailors of the Minnesota. But they knew that they alone—they and their cheese box—stood between the Union and disaster. And, like old Seth, they meant "to do their endeavorest."

So, all night, beneath the iron deck of the Monitor, steam pumps were forcing out the sea-water and sucking in the air. Up through the open hatches came many muffled sounds—the slow throb of engines, the voices of petty officers giving orders, the metallic scrape of shovels in the bunkers, and the rattling fall of coal, the clang of furnace doors, the tramp of feet, the hoisting of powder and eleven-inch shot into the turret, the splash of wet ashes passed up from below and thrown overboard.

Unconscious of the tragedy which had come at Waverley, and of the greater tragedy which was coming, unconscious of the accusation hanging over him, and of the bitter battle Virginia was fighting for his sake, Earl Hamilton was leaning over the rail of the Minnesota, watching the arrival of the Monitor. That day had given him an instant of perfect happiness, cut short with the acute pain of parting; that day had brought disaster to the country which he loved in proportion to the sacrifices he had made for it.

The danger to himself in tomorrow's battle he did not realize, because, sailor-fashion, he did not think of it. The danger to the Union cause, he thought of much and fully realized. So, when the dark turret of the new Ericsson battery appeared, half a mile away, moving over the waves in the light of the great burning, he scanned it eagerly. He knew the tremendous weight of responsibility which now rested upon the queer little ironclad. Could she bear it? Half an hour after she anchored alongside his ship, he received orders from Captain Marston detailing him as pilot of the new craft in the battle expected next morning. It was hardly an officer's duty, but Hamilton knew that, after the treachery of that day, the piloting was of supreme importance. He had the gig lowered, and quickly set foot on the low freeboard of the Monitor. There were no masts, no sails, no bulwarks, no davits, no boats—nothing but a platform on the sea, a platform which here, in this sheltered roadstead, was scarce eighteen inches above the

water-line. Hamilton saw that the whole deck
would be submerged in the rush of the deep-sea
waves.

In the center of the platform was the circular iron
turret, twenty feet in diameter, whose top he could
almost touch with his finger tips. Besides the turret, there was only the pilot-house, rising to the
height of his chest, the smokestack, of which the
top was level with his eyes, the flagstaffs on the
bow and stern, and the standing pipes through
which the air was drawn down to the furnaces, and
to the crew who worked, and ate, and slept below
the water line. It was like going down into a mine
—quarters, magazine, engine-room, cockpit, wardroom, knew no light but that of lamp and lantern.
Worden and his officers were working indefatigably
to get the floating battery in shape for battle, and
Hamilton, after reporting to the commanding officer, examined by himself everything from anchor-
well to propeller. Then he went back to the Minnesota and spent the night getting information
about the Merrimac, comparing the two antagonists
in his mind, weighing their chances, inventing
schemes of attack and defense. Little did he think
as he worked and schemed, that, off there on the
dear old hill, at Waverley, a document was growing, page by page—a document which was officially

13

making the woman he loved a spy and murderess, and making Hamilton himself a traitor to the North.

The light from the Congress ceased after the explosion, the moon traversed the sky and set, and in the black, still hour before the dawn, Hamilton slept. There were yet three hours before the fight.

In the east, intensifying the blackness of the earth, appeared a streak of gray which grew until it glowed, and barred the sky with black and crimson. Water and shores were veiled in mist.

Two sailors on the Monitor's deck were kneeling at the base of the turret, pulling soaked oakum from under it with improvised wire hooks. A third sailor had fallen asleep, face down, on the bolted iron plating of the deck. They were grimy, unshaven, unkempt.

"This is better'n bein' shut in a iron box under water," said one of the men.

"Awful smell down there," agreed the other. "Pete's played out," he observed, glancing at the sleeper. Then he looked at the handful of flabby oakum which he held. "What'll we do with this here stuff? Overboard?"

"Bo's'n said, take it to the wardroom. Next time we strike half a sea we'll get another shower bath below—oakum or no oakum."

The boatswain's mate stumbled up the hatchway upon the deck. He shook himself and drew a deep breath.

"Blamed if I ain't asleep standin' up!" he growled. Then he caught sight of the man asleep lying down. "Hi, there, you lubber!" he shouted, poking with his toes the sleeper's ribs. "What do you mean? Wake up!"

The man stirred, groaned, and rolled asleep again.

"Wake up!" repeated the boatswain's mate, emphasizing the command with a vigorous kick. "Clear for action, you!"

The man rose heavily and grumbled, " 'Tain't much sleep—five minutes in three days."

"You yank that oakum out o' there quick," was the mate's delicate repartee. He examined the iron base of the turret, which was supposed to form a water-tight joint with the great bronze ring let into the deck.

"She's rusted," he observed. "Pass out that oil can."

Seeing that the ports of the turret were closed, he exclaimed, "What the ———! Why ain't that port-stopper open?" He ran up the ladder to the top of the turret, leaned down into the hatchway and shouted, "Trice up that port-stopper. Are you afraid of catching cold in there?"

"There ain't enough of us. She's too heavy," came a sepulchral protest from within the iron tower.

"Heavy be blowed. Get ahold there." The mate disappeared through the hatch and presently the great pendulum port-stopper moved clear of the port. A yellow beam of light came through the opening and was lost in the spreading daylight.

"Pass out that oil can." An arm thrust out the specified article, which was taken by one of the men outside. The mate's head appeared, "Oil that hemp and rub rust. Clear round." The mate vanished.

From the hatchway emerged two officers and a trim seaman, the latter carrying two folded flags. The officers filled their lungs and looked about.

"Run them right up, John." The sailor saluted, and going to the fore, bent on the Stars and Stripes, being careful not to let one silk fold touch the deck.

To the eastward, the two officers, Greene and Webber, could see the black hulls of the Roanoke and St. Lawrence, looming above the water; beyond the frigates they could make out through the mists the bastions of the fort.

"Where is the Merrimac?" asked Webber, who carried no glass.

"She must lie off here in the heavier mist," said the other, pointing his glass to the southwest.

"There you can see the rip-raps—the Merrimac is under Sewall's Point, still farther to the right." He handed over his glass to Webber.

Here and there the mist was wavering and breaking.

"There she is now," cried Webber, as he caught a glimpse of a great black citadel upon the water. "Here, off the port quarter about four miles." He returned the glass to Greene, who also saw.

"I wonder if she's got up steam?" he said, glancing at their own smokestack, whence a black cloud was pouring up.

"I can't see whether that's mist or smoke," said Webber.

"It's mist," answered Greene, after a moment. The sun was striking the fog now, and curling it up in great white wreaths.

"The lucky dogs are asleep," observed Webber, taking the glass from his eyes.

"No sleep for us," said Greene.

"The gas in that engine-room was death on lungs," commented Webber.

"And the sound in that anchor-well resembled the death groans of twenty men," added Greene. "It was the most horrible, dismal sound I ever heard."

The Merrimac could now be seen plainly, and

Webber, allowing for distance, and estimating her size, exclaimed, "Jove, she's big! It's David and Goliath today."

Lieutenant Worden, a large man with a very long beard, square-cut, came up the hatchway. He was calm, but very earnest—with the air of a man who is keeping many things in mind for instant use. The officers saluted, and Worden observed the Merrimac.

"Steam not yet up on her?" he said, and without waiting for an answer, added, with satisfaction, "We're ahead of her. Lieutenant Hamilton not yet come?" he asked, still looking at the Merrimac.

"Not yet, sir," answered Greene.

"What time is it, Greene?" asked the commanding officer, still looking through his glass.

"Seven-fifteen."

"Hamilton should come," he said, turning and slipping his glass into its case. "He saw the Merrimac in action. He knows her tactics. I've been counting on his suggestions before we begin."

"I just now heard them lower a boat on the Minnesota, sir. It's probably Hamilton."

From the distant funnel of the Merrimac curled up a wreath of smoke.

"There's the smoke," said Worden, quickly.

"She's getting up steam." A boat, with two rowers and Lieutenant Hamilton came round the stern of the Minnesota. Evidently the findings of the courtmartial had not yet caused Hamilton's arrest.

Without haste, and speaking very precisely, Worden began giving orders for the impending action. "Lieutenant Greene," he said, "you will command the turret, taking sixteen men to work the guns and machinery. Mr. Webber, you will command the powder division on the berth deck. Station the paymaster and my clerk, Toffey, to pass orders from the pilot-house."

Hamilton stepped aboard and saluted. Worden returned the salute, and continued, in the same precise voice:

"Lieutenant Hamilton will take his place with me, in the pilot-house. We will remain on deck for observation until the last moment. Lieutenant Greene, tell Mr. Stodder that he is to take charge of the wheel for revolving the turret and its engine. Give Mr. Stimers my compliments, and ask him if he will kindly help you and Stodder, as emergencies arise." Chief Engineer Stodder was a passenger, who had already volunteered to serve in any capacity. "Bo's'n!" called Worden, down the hatchway.

"Aye, aye, sir," came the deep response from below.

"Get your men forward to the anchor windlass. Be ready to weigh at a moment's notice."

"Aye, aye, sir," repeated the hearty voice.

"Lieutenant," called Worden to Greene, who had turned to go, "tell Stodder to try the revolving machinery at once. To your posts, gentlemen! You know that on the fight we make depends the fate of all these frigates, our seaboard cities, and perhaps the very existence of the Union."

There was a tightening about the lips and a gleam of resolution in the eyes of the young officers, as they saluted and turned away. It was a short speech and a simple, but Thucydides could have invented none to make men fight better. Among the men ran a terser sentence with a lower meaning and a fiercer emotion—"Remember the Cumberland!"

Worden alone with Hamilton, gave his brother officer a nod of good will. "We are lucky, sir," he said, "to have today an officer who knows the water. From what I hear, those pilots should swing at the yard arm."

"I got the scoundrels their berths, too," said Hamilton, disgustedly. "I would have sworn some of those fellows could not be induced to do an underhanded thing. Of course, they are natives of this section, and their sympathies run the other way."

"You saw the Merrimac in action, Lieutenant?" said Worden, coming quickly to the all-important question. "Can we beat her?"

"If this machine works as it's meant to, we can beat her by maneuvering," answered Hamilton. "Her smokestack's all shot up, her fires will have little draft, and she'll be slower than yesterday."

"What's her speed?"

"Five knots yesterday; less today."

"And her draft?"

"Twenty-two feet. Ours must be about ten?"

"Exactly."

"The water is but eighteen where we are now," said Hamilton. "We can skim all around her, dodge her broadsides, and draw off to shoal water if she tries to board. That overcomes the advantage of her big crew."

"We're a small target, too," added Worden. "The four guns of her broadside are therefore no better than our single shot. We fire but one of our two guns at a time. She has no solid shot?"

"Nothing but shells. Six-inch rifles and nine-inch Dahlgrens."

"Against our eleven-inch solid shot!" exclaimed

Worden. He had been led to believe the Merrimac's ordinance heavier.

A great black cloud was by this time issuing from the mutilated smokestack of the Merrimac. Instead of drawing strongly from the top, it came puffing out through the great shot holes, which had been very imperfectly closed.

With the puffing of a small engine below deck, and some scraping, the turret started to revolve. Worden observed it carefully.

"It doesn't start smoothly," he said, "the water came under it in a perfect cascade; the vertical shaft and the cogs are rusted. But it will work unless the Merrimac's shells stop it."

"Dare we ram her?" asked Hamilton. "Will our cutwater stand it?"

"It will," answered Worden, "and our hull is as solid as rock."

"We should try to smash her propellor."

"How about the Merrimac's ram?"

"It was cast iron and tore loose. She left it in the Cumberland." As Hamilton spoke, he saw a boat from shore head toward the Monitor, but paid no attention.

"How deep is her propellor?" asked Worden, thinking of the nearness to the surface of the Monitor's bow.

"I tried to find out during the night," answered Hamilton. Worden reflected that his pilot had not been wasting time. "The man I depended on had not come when I left the Minnesota. I gave orders for him to follow me here, if he came in time."

"We'll try your plan, anyway," said Worden. The click-clack of oars between thole-pins attracted his attention toward the shore. "Perhaps that's your man," he suggested.

"It doesn't look like him," said Hamilton. "There's one more thing I thought of. How much powder is there, sir, in one of our charges?"

"Fifteen pounds."

Hamilton shook his head. "Can't we use more?" he asked. He knew the charge for each piece was prescribed, and he looked significantly at Worden to see if he were willing to exceed the authorized charge.

"Strictest orders against it," replied Worden, with unmoved face.

"It won't pierce her," said Hamilton, disappointedly.

"Are you sure?"

"Perfectly."

"Then we will have to shoot at her guns. I must tell Greene this." Worden ascended the turret and leaned over the hatchway, talking to Greene inside.

Hamilton took another look at the man in the boat, who was now within hail. He saw only the back, but the back was unmistakable.

"Willis!" he exclaimed. Willis it was, and as he brought his boat alongside, Hamilton greeted him with ejaculations of disgust.

"What the hell do you mean by coming aboard this machine?" he demanded. "There's no sense in your risking your neck for that newspaper of yours. Stay on shore; you can see better what's going on. Nobody knows what this thing's going to do."

Willis preserved the silence of the Sphinx. He made fast his boat, stopping as he did so to scan curiously another small boat just leaving the shore. "Has anybody made you any trouble since last night?" he asked, straightening up.

"No. Why?" replied Hamilton.

"I've some papers for you to look at," Willis answered inconsequentially. He took carefully from his pocket the message Von Benzinger had given to Harlan. One corner of each paper was stained dark red. "Be careful," he said, handing over Von Benzinger's dispatch to Wool. "Don't let it blow away. It's valuable."

Willis was relieved to find that no other messenger of Von Benzinger's had secured Hamilton's arrest. He began to think they had not found Harlan, in which case Von Benzinger would believe his dispatches had reached their destination, and would take no further step.

Hamilton glancing at the official heading, saw that Waverley was now the headquarters of a Federal brigade. Then he read—

"'I strongly suspect the Virginian, Lieutenant Earl Hamilton, U. S. N., of being in communication with Richmond, and of inducing pilots to ground ships.'"

Hamilton's gray eyes blazed with fury. "Who is the pup?" he shouted, and his eye sought the signature. "Hugo von Benzinger!" he exclaimed, with amazement. "General von Benzinger? What does he mean?" The tone of fierce inquiry in the last words boded ill for Von Benzinger if he should be forced to answer in person.

"Read along," said Willis, "and keep as cool as you can."

"'The bearer of this has strong confirmation, which he will lay before you,'" read Hamilton. "Who's the bearer—where did you get this?" he demanded.

"The bearer was Harlan," replied Willis. "I got it from him."

"This?" said Hamilton, incredulously. "Harlan carrying Von Benzinger's message? Damn it, man, drop your theatrical mystery, and out with what you know."

"The next sentence explains about Harlan," said Willis, unruffled by his friend's heat.

" 'He has already rendered important secret services.' Oh, yes," said Hamilton, bitterly, "to both sides. Did he give you this?"

"Yes," said Willis, slowly. "Not willingly, though."

"What did you do?"

"I shot him."

"Shot him!" For an instant Hamilton looked extreme disapproval. "You shouldn't have done it," he blurted out. Then a new thought struck him. "Good God, old fellow, you did it to save me. Thanks, thanks, for your splendid friendship, but you shouldn't have done it; you shouldn't have done it."

"Harlan deserved it," said Willis.

"I know, I know, but—did you kill him?"

"No," said Willis, "he fell at my shot, but picked himself up afterward. Look at the next thing in this truthful epistle." As Hamilton read, Willis looked anxiously at the boat coming from shore. There were two men in it; it came slowly, and it was headed for the Monitor. "Von Benzinger's accusation," thought Willis.

" 'Virginia Eggleston, of Waverley plantation, is probably his accomplice. Am watching her,' " read Hamilton. "The hound!" he exclaimed. "He'd better not say anything against her!"

Over at Sewall's Point the Merrimac was now moving, swinging her ponderous length until she should head toward the Minnesota. Worden came from the turret toward the main hatchway. He looked curiously at Willis.

"Does your news bear on the fight, Lieutenant?" he asked.

"No, sir," said Hamilton, "it's an infamous lie about me and the woman I love."

"No time for that now, Lieutenant," said Worden, a little sharply.

"Lieutenant Worden, she is in danger; I must have a moment to think—to form a plan. It takes fifteen minutes to wind the Merrimac. She won't be in good range for half an hour." Hamilton's earnestness appealed to Worden.

"Just so you keep your nerve steady for the battle," he said, relenting. "I give you till we weigh anchor. Remember your duty, sir." The commander of the Monitor went below.

"Look here, Hamilton," said Willis. "Do you see that boat coming this way."

"Yes," said the Lieutenant.

"Now, ten to one that's an order for your arrest on this suspicion of Von Benzinger's. That's why I came here—to block his game. It's just like him to wait till the last minute, so the Monitor won't have time to get another pilot."

"But, why?" asked Hamilton, dazed. "He wouldn't want to do that."

"He wouldn't?" sniffed Willis. "I haven't time to explain. Von Benzinger's a Confederate—or will be if this cheese box is beaten. He designed the Merrimac."

Hamilton stared blankly.

"This proves it," said Willis, handing over the note which was half cipher. All that Hamilton could read was, of course, the open writing at the bottom.

To Lieutenant E. H.,
     On Minnesota.
  Your proposal concerning pilots is approved. Will count on you. Merrimac will attack on seventh or eighth.
          Franklin Buchanan, C. S. N.

"Great guns, man!" ejaculated Hamilton, startled at the words which seemed to fasten the guilt of corrupting the pilots conclusively upon himself. "That's damned queer proof of *Von Benzinger's* treachery."

"Von Benzinger wrote it himself. He bribed the

pilots. That's why he forged this. Harlan was taking it to Buchanan. Buchanan was to copy it. Then Harlan would go to Wool with it. Wool knows Buchanan's writing. It would have finished you. Devilish clever scheme, eh?"

"Oh, devilish," said Earl. He somehow failed to appreciate, as Willis did, the aesthetic quality of the thing. "What's this cipher stuff?" he asked.

"That's the kernel of the nut," said Willis. "It's the most diabolical cipher I ever tackled, and I knew practically what it said, too." With innocent pride Willis read off the cipher:

Flag Officer Franklin Buchanan,
    Commanding Merrimac.

Monitor in Roads, and will fight you tomorrow. Board her, lash her, cover turret with tarpaulins; throw in hand grenades.

Von B.

"Better catch her before he boards her," said Hamilton, grimly. "So that's Von Benzinger! Well, Willis, you know how much I owe you. I take back what I said about shooting Harlan. If it hadn't been for you, I can see where Virginia and I would be. And you've done the country a service in blocking the scheme to leave the Monitor without a pilot. Now it's simple. With that cipher, and your proof as to what Harlan really was, you can finish Von Benzinger. You must go straight

14

to Wool. Why didn't you go there in the first place?"

"I thought Von Benzinger would find out Harlan didn't get to the fort. Then he'd invent something else to stop you. The surest place to intercept him was here. Once into the battle you're safe—so is the Monitor."

"Thanks," said Hamilton.

"Who's in that boat, anyway?" asked Willis.

"It can't be Henderson, can it?"

"By Jimtown, it is."

"Bad news from Virginia," muttered Earl.

The man rowing Henderson's boat brought her alondside and caught hold of the deck.

"What's wrong, Squire?" asked Hamilton, as the Squire stepped gingerly aboard.

"Sir, you are a Federal officer," said Henderson. "You are a Federal officer, but Mrs. Poynter says that Miss Virginia's life depends on your comin' right away to Waverley."

"What has happened, man? Speak quick."

"I'm afraid, sir—I hate to say—I cannot believe that a lady of her refinement—"

"For God's sake, what is it?"

"I'm afraid, Earl," said the Squire—the old name coming to his lips in his emotion—"I'm afraid she killed Lafe Harlan. It must have been accidental."

"Who says she did?" demanded Hamilton, fierce-ly.

"General von Benzinger."

Hamilton gave an inarticulate snarl, as if of a great caged animal.

"The sentry said he thought she did it—it looked like it to him. Harlan was lying shot through the lung at her feet, an' her pistol was still warm right where she dropped it beside her. And Harlan himself, when Von Benzinger asked him who shot him, said 'Virginia'—I came in just as he said it, and it was the last word he ever spoke."

"So he's dead," mused Willis.

"The blackguard!" burst out Hamilton. "The coward! The ——! My God! How could the man do that? Lafe couldn't do that!"

"I heard him say it," reasserted the Squire, mournfully.

"Did Lafe understand Von Benzinger's question?" asked Hamilton. "*I* would have died with her name on my lips." It was a great, illuminating touch of charity. Hamilton had put himself in Harlan's place.

"I never thought of that," said the Squire, his face brightening. No one else had thought of it till then—the eye witnesses of the tragedy had been so convinced of Virginia's guilt by what they had heard and seen that Harlan's dying word had only added assurance to a certainty. And the hope entertained by some that the shooting would be proved accidental was removed when the evidence brought out the strong motives Virginia had for intercepting Harlan's messages.

"I shot Harlan myself," said Willis, abruptly.

"You!" exclaimed the bewildered Squire. "So you're the murderer?"

"That's not the word, Squire. We fought."

"You fought? Lafe Harlan was the best shot in Virginia."

Willis took off his hat and showed a red line on the side of his head. "An inch makes a big difference sometimes," he observed.

"When is the trial to be, Squire?" asked Hamilton, thinking, of course, that he and Willis would have plenty of time to show what Von Benzinger was, and establish Virginia's innocence.

"They tried her late last night," replied the Squire.

"What! What was it—the verdict?" asked Hamilton, with horror.

The Merrimac loomed large now—less than a mile away.

"I heard—" began Henderson. He looked at Hamilton and stopped.

"Tell me, man!"

"I heard she was condemned."

"Condemned!" groaned Hamilton.

"When I left," said Henderson, "they were sending the findings of the courtmartial to the fort for General Wool to sign."

There was a flash and puff of smoke in one of the Merrimac's bow ports. The shell crashed into the stern of the Minnesota. Burning splinters were thrown upon the forward deck of the Monitor.

"Weigh anchor," came the deep and long-drawn call of the boatswain, below the deck. Henderson scrambled into his boat; the man with him cast off and rowed as fast as he could, westward, toward Newport News.

"To the fort, Willis!" said Hamilton, with intense earnestness. "Her life depends on you. You have everything—cipher—story—all." The Minnesota's stern-chasers opened on the Merrimac.

"Lieutenant Hamilton!" The voice was Worden's, coming through the narrow sight-hole of the pilot-house. "Dismiss that boat, sir, and to your post."

A second shell from the Merrimac screamed overhead, and striking halfway between the Monitor and the shore, threw up a great column of water. Willis stepped into his boat. Hamilton gave him the precious cipher and a warm pressure of the hand. The Lieutenant cast off the painter, and Willis started eastward toward the fort.

"Show Wool your proof," shouted Hamilton, running toward the stern as the boat moved off. "Tell him you killed Harlan, and who Harlan was. Get orders for Von Benzinger's arrest."

"All right, old chap," called out Willis, cheerily. "You save the Union, and I'll save the girl."

Hamilton realized that Willis had the whole situation more clearly in hand than he had himself. Willis knew what to do, and would do it. Hamilton was the only man left on the deck, and now the Monitor began to move. He must get to the pilot-house quickly. The Monitor, circling the Minnesota, passed close to Henderson's slow-moving scow.

"Tell Mrs. Poynter that Willis will clear Virginia," he shouted. Just as he started down the hatchway, there was a flash in the starboard port of the Merrimac. The gun bore on neither the Minnesota nor the Monitor. Under the overhanging bow-sprit of the Minnesota, Hamilton saw the exploding shell knock Willis' boat into kindling wood. The waters closed above it. The Monitor passed on, the great hull of the frigate shut the spot from sight.

"Willis!" groaned Hamilton. The shell had taken his best friend. A second sudden thought cut deeper yet—"Virginia! That shell as good as kills her, too." Back upon the deck sprang Earl He rushed to the Monitor's stern to catch another glimpse of Willis. Too late—the view from the Monitor was cut off by the frigate's bow. He shouted to the men on the Minnesota to look beyond and tell him what they saw. In vain, her crew were busy, the roar of the Minnesota's guns drowned his voice.

The Monitor, having completed a half circle about the frigate, was already headed squarely for the Merrimac. Now her engines stopped. Was it for him—the pilot? What use to see more? What hope was there for Willis? Had he not seen the shell strike square?

"Henderson!" he shouted. "Come back! I must go with you to Waverley!" But Henderson was either beyond hearing, or he would not come back. Frantically Earl tore off his blouse. It was only a mile to shore.

"Lieutenant Hamilton!" thundered Worden's voice behind him. Hamilton faced his commanding officer. "This ship is in action, sir," said Worden.

"They are murdering her—I'm going," came the reply.

Worden leveled his pistol. "Leave this ship and I shoot," he said, firmly.

"Shoot, then!" panted Hamilton, "I'm going."

"Man, are you mad?" cried Worden, lowering his pistol. "The battle depends on you. The Union depends on you. What can we do without a pilot? Will you leave us without a pilot?" The words did not reach Hamilton's mind. "Lieutenant!" Worden spoke as to a sleep-walker. "Hamilton! You're trying to desert."

Hamilton was staggered. "Desert!" he repeated. Worden had found the master word. "I'll not desert," said Hamilton.

One ray of hope flashed into his despair. The battle over, he would rush to Waverley. Ah! Would he be too late?

CHAPTER XVI.

THE DUEL OF IRONCLADS.

Boom!

Von Benzinger stirred uneasily where he still slept, his head upon the table.

Boom! Boom! Boom! Boom!

He sat upright in the chair. "The guns of the Merrimac," he murmured. "I cannot be mistaken."

Boom! The tone was deep, strong and full. It sounded like a base note struck in accord with the lighter ones that had gone before.

Boom! Boom! Boom! Boom! The Merrimac again. The General sprang to his feet and turned to the window. It was broad day, and a mocking-bird, alighting in a pine tree near by, poured forth a volume of liquid notes.

Boom! Once more that single roll of ominous thunder. The windows rattled with the sound.

"Thunders of hell! I have slept, and the battle is on." He looked at his watch. It was five minutes past eight, and the findings of the courtmartial had not gone. They should have been at the fort two hours ago. "Orderly!" Von Benzinger sprang to the door, and tried to throw it open. "Has the devil deserted me?" he cried, savagely. Then, remembering having locked the door after receiving the result of the courtmartial, he turned the key and strode into the hall.

"Orderly!" he called, his voice having an unfamiliar tone, even in his own ears.

A soldier stepped into the hall from the gallery, saluted and stood at attention.

"My compliments to Lieutenant Edwards—I wish to see him at once."

The guard saluted, and withdrew.

"To fall asleep at such a time," he muttered, as he turned once more into the room, and hurrying to the table, opened the findings. His eye ran over the pages. Evidence of Von Benzinger—he smiled grimly—of the sentry—of Mrs. Poynter—of Henderson—of Estelle—ah, here it is. "We find Virginia Eggleston guilty of conspiring, with Lieutenant Hamilton, of the Union frigate Minnesota, to corrupt the pilots and wreck the fleet, and of the murder of Lafe Harlan, a Union messenger, and we fix the penalty at death. We also recommend that Lieutenant Hamilton be immediately placed

The duel of ironclads.

under arrest and tried for treason." It was there—everything necessary to have kept Hamilton from the Monitor.

Boom!

The gun again! How big and threatening it sounded. In imagination, he saw the great solid shot striking the Merrimac, and he staggered as though he himself had received the blow.

Boom! Boom! Boom! Boom!

It was the smaller voice of the Merrimac, replying with her four-gun broadside. The detonations were smaller, pitched in a higher key than those from the Monitor.

"There is a difference. I shall know how the battle goes by the sound of the guns," he said, his eyes flashing, as the spirit of the conflict caught fire in his soldier's heart. Then he turned once more to the documents.

He had barely seated himself when Edwards appeared at the door. "Good morning, Lieutenant!" The voice was quiet now. The iron will of the man had conquered. The nerves so lately in mutiny had been overcome, bent down, chained, and the master ruled alone.

"Good morning, sir. You have orders for me?"

"Yes. What is that firing in the Roads?"

"The Monitor has attacked the Merrimac, sir. The first gun was fired ten minutes ago."

"Can you see the action from here?"

"Fairly well, sir, from the housetop."

"Is there a way up there?"

"Yes, sir. A stairway from the second landing. Geary and I were up just now."

"Good. You will prepare to ride to the fort with papers of importance for General Wool. Take a guard of six men—of the right kind. You understand?"

"Yes, sir. Have you any orders for breakfast?"

"Tell some of the servants to bring coffee to the dining-room—no—in the library." The court-martial had been held in the dining-room. He did not like the thoughts of it. "Where's Geary?"

"At breakfast, sir."

"Very well. I'll send to him later. When you are ready, call here for the papers."

Boom!

General von Benzinger started, as the roar of the big gun rolled through the house. It was followed immediately by the four shots of the Merrimac, one following the other in rapid succession.

"Why does the Merrimac fire in that order?" cried the General, springing up and starting toward the door.

"We noticed that, sir, and Geary concluded that as the Monitor was such a small mark the bigger boat fired one gun after another as they came in range."

"Quite likely." The General was cool again. "That will do. In half an hour everything will be ready for you."

Edwards saluted and retired.

Alone once more, Von Benzinger took up the findings of the courtmartial and went over each page with care, stopping occasionally to comment on some point in the evidence that pleased him. The witnesses had told their stories reluctantly; this was manifest from the questions and answers, a point to argue against the accused, as the arch conspirator knew full well. He noted the rambling and irrelevant replies of Virginia—replies as of one talking in a dream. There was a big blot in one place, on the otherwise neat manuscript, and immediately following it, the line: "The prisoner fainted, and was taken from the room by Surgeon Cuthbertson."

"Lieutenant Harper is careless!" said the General, coolly eyeing the inkspot. When he came to the clause which recommended the immediate arrest of Hamilton, he frowned, and bit his lip.

"If I hadn't been such a fool to fall asleep, he

would be in irons now, instead of out there helping Ericsson, curse him! But if he wins, what of it? That will not save the life of his fair Virginia. If he loses, I do not care. They can both go free, for I shall be master of the sea—their poor lives I can afford to spare." And the plotter smiled grimly at his suggested generosity.

"A very pretty complication, Monsieur Hamilton," he mused. "I wonder how it would be solved if you knew that by a single turn of a screw you might save the life of the girl you love, and your own as well. That if you refuse to make that turn, the stipulations of this contract will be carried out to the end." He tapped the findings significantly. "But you do not know, and the Merrimac must fight her way to victory, or—or General von Benzinger remain what he is, a Union spy-catcher."

Boom!

"Damn the gun! It has a voice like a volcano to shake the earth." But the Merrimac's reply was quick and sharp, and the ring of her guns had a tone of cheer to the man who sat there in the blue uniform of a Union General, praying to his pagan gods success for the Southern ram.

"The Merrimac will win," he thought. "But if she doesn't, there must be no slip in this evidence." One by one he took up the articles introduced at the trial, and examined them in connection with the final report.

Exhibit A. Letter of Hamilton to Virginia, found in her room, announcing his safety after the battle.

Exhibit B. Letter of Virginia to Hamilton, warning him of the suspicions aroused concerning the pilots.

Exhibit C. Richmond Whig, containing advertisement of Harlan's connection with the Federal Government.

Exhibit D. Copy of dispatch, written by Von Benzinger to Wool, charging Hamilton with treachery, and given to Harlan for delivery.

Exhibit E. Pistol, acknowledged by Virginia to be hers, and found empty at her feet, when Harlan was shot.

Exhibit F. Bullet taken from Harlan's dead body, and which fitted the pistol, marked Exhibit E.

Exhibit G. Bullet moulds in which the ball was run, and which were proved to be the property of Virginia Eggleston.

Exhibit H. Sketch of Waverley, indicating the spot where Harlan was shot, and position of Virginia Eggleston ; the sentry, who heard the shot ; the pistol and the body of Harlan.

Having placed all these mute witnesses against

Virginia in a compact package, General von Benzinger sealed it, and addressed it to General Wool. Then hurriedly turning over the leaves of the evidence, he read again that of the sentry. After describing the location, where he was posted, and the distance he was required to cover, his evidence said:

"It was nearly eleven o'clock. I was at the end of my post, farthest from the house, when I saw a man run across the road and through the gate. I ordered him to halt, and ran in his direction. He paid no attention to my order, but ran on straight toward the house. I called again, 'Halt, or I fire,' but he ran on. As I brought my gun to my shoulder to fire, he was in direct range of an open door of the house, and, in the light thrown from within, I saw a woman standing on the lawn, near the steps that led up to the gallery. I could not fire without danger of hitting her. Just as he came within a few feet of her, I heard a pistol shot, and saw the man fall. I do not know whether she fired the shot or not, but it came from her direction."

From Geary's evidence, he read, "When I reached the spot, General von Benzinger and several other people had come from the house. I heard the General ask the man who shot him, and he said, 'Virginia.' I saw General von Benzinger pick up a pistol at her feet and examine it. He then handed it to me, and asked me to do the same. It was not loaded, but there was burned powder about the muzzle, and the barrel was warm, as if it had been recently fired. General von Benzinger ordered the woman placed under arrest."

"Perfect," thought Von Benzinger, as he folded the sheets, placed them in an envelope, and prepared to seal them up. "Was it my pistol that was accidentally discharged, my fair Virginia? Ugh! The man's appearance was enough to make any finger press too hard upon the trigger. Very well. It is the keystone in the arch of this temple I have erected for my preservation. It is the fate of war, fair rebel—love and war. You scorned me; you preferred a miserable sailor to the man whose brain has overthrown the systems of centuries, whose genius has created a new navy, whose Merrimac—"

Boom!

"The Monitor again. I had almost forgotten you, Monsieur Ericsson. Ha! What do you here, Madam? This is my headquarters. You should be announced." He arose hurriedly, and, blowing the flame from the burning wax in his hand, glowered at Mrs. Poynter, standing within the door.

"General von Benzinger," said the widow, her

voice trembling with anxiety and emotion. "What are they going to do to Virginia?"

"She has been tried, Mrs. Poynter."

"Oh, don't I know that, poor dear. But she is innocent of these horrible charges, innocent as an angel!"

"I trust so, Mrs. Poynter."

"I wish I might believe you. What did that ghostly tribunal decide?"

"That I cannot tell you."

"Have those papers anything to do with it? Is that their verdict?" cried Mrs. Poynter, taking a step toward the table, and indicating the half-sealed envelope.

"The findings went to General Wool an hour ago," said the General, inventing a lie to save time. "This is my statement of the case—in fact, a plea for mercy. The prisoner is young, pretty, daughter of an old Virginia family—there may be some mistake. Wool should be in no haste to approve the findings of the court, should they prove prejudicial to Miss Eggleston. Merely suggestions, Mrs. Poynter, but I do not doubt Wool will consider them." Intrigue fascinated him, and he wished not to be troubled with Mrs. Poynter's pleadings and demands. The battle in the Roads interested him above everything else. An occasional boom from the Monitor, followed by the fourfold roll of the Merrimac, told him neither ship had, as yet, gained any practical advantage. Once these papers were on their way to Wool, the fight should have his undivided attention.

Mrs. Poynter's troubled face cleared with his statement concerning Virginia. His words were reassuring, and gave her hope. Von Benzinger was the only one in the place who could offer help, and she had looked for frowns and a curt dismissal from him. To find him already engaged in trying to save Virginia aroused her liveliest gratitude, and she hastened to express it.

"How noble of you, General. I shall never forget it as long as I live. I am sure Wool will listen to you. He is a kind man, although he is such a stickler for military justice. Senator Poynter and he were good friends. Why, perhaps he would listen to me. I'll order a horse and ride over immediately."

Here was a danger Von Benzinger had not counted on. His diplomacy had proved a boomerang. She must not go to the fort, that was certain.

"Your thought is a good one, Mrs. Poynter, but impracticable. There is a battle going on in the Roads; military operations of the greatest importance are being considered by the heads of departments, and you would find admittance to General Wool difficult, if not impossible."

"I am sure he would see me," declared the widow, with emphasis.

"It would be a tedious wait at best, and the audience might come too late. The road from here to the fort is crowded with soldiers, foot and horse, artillery, transportation trains, and natives drunken with yesterday's victory. A dangerous ride for a man. Impossible for a woman."

"But I must see General Wool," she exclaimed, tears starting from her eyes. "I would risk anything to get Virginia's release."

"Why not write, Mrs. Poynter?"

"It would take a letter a year to reach him!" she cried, hysterically.

"You might send it with this," he said, a tigerish gleam in his eye. "If what you write were slipped in here before I finish sealing the package, it would go directly. Edwards is waiting for it now."

"You're a genius," cried the widow, her quick sympathies making her an easy victim. "What shall I say?" as she seated herself at the table, and took up a pen—'My dear General Wool'—There, I'm so nervous I can't think."

"Why not write: 'I endorse every word here

written by General von Benzinger,' and sign it, Ready in a moment, Edwards. Make haste, Mrs. Poynter, my orderly is waiting."

"Here it is, General. 'I endorse every word here written by General von Benzinger. Cora Poynter.' Shall I slip it in the envelope?" She would have caught up the package, but Von Benzinger quickly interposed, took the slip from her fingers, deftly ran it through the opening, sealed it, and then, turning to Mrs. Poynter, said, with great coolness:

"It will reach the General safely, never fear, Mrs. Poynter. You will excuse me now. I must have a word with my aide."

He held the door open, bowed politely, as she passed out, and then, catching up the exhibits and the findings, gave them to Edwards, with instructions to guard them with his life; place them in the hands of none but General Wool, and to wait for Wool's reply.

"An added strength!" He laughed aloud at the thought. "The clever widow endorses the chain of evidence I forged with such care. And she declares Wool to be famous for military justice. Even his nature favors me. He will approve the findings. I am safe, however the battle goes."

From the distant waters came the reverberative

roar of the Monitor. A moment later the Merrimac replied.

One, two, three—the fourfold roar was broken. The Merrimac had lost a gun. "Diable!" exclaimed Von Benzinger, and hastily mounted the stairs to the roof.

Virginia knelt by the window, looking out upon the battle in the Roads. The hours of endless anguish had swept away her strength, and her eyes seemed unusually large and lustrous in the setting of her pale cheeks. The endless hours! She had lived years since yesterday morning—happy morning, when her girl troubles seemed so great. Through the gathering smoke came the roll of the Merrimac's guns. How different from yesterday. Then the guns of this new hope of the South were drowned by the roar of more than a hundred cannon thundering against its iron sides. Now there was only the roll of its broadside—broken by that one infrequent gun which her heart told her was the Monitor.

Boom! How deep it was; how commanding! Was Hamilton on that ship? If she only knew what had happened—what was happening. Was Earl accused? Did he, too, chafe in confinement, listening to those guns? Must he, too, wait, powerless, while his trial went on, without a chance to tell the truth and prove his innocence? "Oh, Earl!" she cried. "You are at least spared the bitterest thought—you do not know the fate that threatens me."

Again the roll of the Merrimac. She had counted the shots over and over again. It relieved her mind. One, two, three, four—no, the fourth was not there. Perhaps the man at that gun had been shot at his post. And Earl, if he had escaped Von Benzinger, and was on the Monitor, that might be his fate. The Merrimac was invincible, pitiless, like the mind that made it—rigid—cruel, not to be overcome. Was it not better so? If the Merrimac should be destroyed, the endless war would grind on and on—men's cut and shattered bodies must fall by thousands, and the hearts of wives and mothers quiver with the pain that is worse than death. If the Merrimac should win, the war would end, the South achieve her independence. If the Merrimac should win, Von Benzinger would go to the Con-federates, his treachery be known, and she be free. But Earl—yes, best for him, too. Best for him even to die in this fight than to live and win it. For, if the Merrimac be beaten, Von Benzinger must stay and she must die, and Earl be accused of treason—dishonored—shot. Oh, strange, strange, strange! Best for her country, best for herself, best for Earl, best for all, that Von Benzinger should triumph; that evil should prevail.

Down in the yard the soldiers were hurrying to and fro, saddling and unsaddling horses, shouting orders, or riding swiftly away. Other horsemen came at intervals, bearing messages which they delivered to the guards at the door, and then dashed madly away again. Once in a while she could hear the voice of Von Benzinger, giving some quick command.

A light breeze blowing off shore swept the smoke of battle out to sea and revealed the strange ships, like two sea-monsters matched in deadly conflict, now charging upon each other with fearful roars and flashes of flame, now withdrawing, circling, alert to rush in again upon the first point of vantage. Now the smaller one went puffing round and round its more formidable antagonist, sending out an occasional shot with a mighty roar that shook the earth. The Merrimac, like a giant dragon, turning more slowly, answered each new challenge of her quicker foe with all the guns she could bring to bear. At first there were four on each side. The dragon's teeth, Von Benzinger called them. An eleven-inch solid shot from the Monitor, planted squarely in the mouth of one of these, had split it half way to the breech. On the opposite side another had been dismounted. But the beast fought on, sullen, revengeful, waiting to catch her lighter adversary in the deeper water, run her down, and crush her to the bottom. Along the shore, officers sat on their horses, anxiously watching the fight. Thousands upon thousands of soldiers and civilians crowded down to the water's edge to witness the thrilling encounter. Not a battery manned, nor a ship moving in the bay—only those two iron monsters out there in the Roads, lashing the water to a foam, puffing, bellowing, charging, ramming, retiring and charging again—the steel-helmeted ideas of two men, Ericsson and Von Benzinger, fighting the duel of a nation, fighting for the supremacy of the sea.

Suddenly a shell struck squarely the pilot-house of the Monitor. The iron top, like the cover of a cistern, flew up and fell back again. The Monitor drifted aimlessly—as though she had lost her mind. Then she turned and ran in toward shore. A shout went up from the Confederate fleet lying in the James. "The Yankee cheese box is quitting! She's whipped! She's whipped!" and they fired pistols and guns, and danced on the decks for joy.

Every heart of the Federal forces stood still. Messages flashed over the wires to Washington, "Prepare to dam the Potomac." An officer came dashing up to Waverley, and, swinging from his horse, ran up the steps to the house. Two orderlies rode through the gate toward their quarters.

"What's wrong with the Monitor?" inquired the guard, pacing back and forth under Virginia's window, as one of the men trotted past.

"One of her officer's wounded. Some say her commander, Worden; some say her pilot, Hamilton. They're bringing him ashore."

"Is that all? Then the boat ain't whipped?"

"That's what they say," and the man spurred on.

Hamilton! Then he was on the boat. He had not been arrested. But he was wounded, perhaps dying. She must go to him. She forgot she was a prisoner, forgot the battle, forgot everything but the words of the soldier. "One of the officers wounded—some say Hamilton." She ran to the door. It was locked. Outside she heard the steady tramp, tramp, tramp of the sentinel, pacing along the hall. Then she heard Black Mammie's voice, mellow and soft and pleading.

"O, Lawd, don' let no ha'm come ter ma po' honey chile. Frow aroun' huh yo' tectin' a'ms, O, Lawd! Don' let no ha'm come ter ma po' honey!"

"Save him, save Earl. O, God of Truth, save and protect him!"

The proud Virginia girl stood with clasped hands and head humbly bowed, joining in the prayer of the black slave to the Author of All.

CHAPTER XVII.

THE DEATH WARRANT.

When Von Benzinger reached the housetop, the two boats were scarcely twenty yards apart, the Monitor swiftly bearing down upon the Merrimac. The General quickly adjusted his glasses. He saw the Monitor swerve to the left, closing upon her adversary. Her turret revolved until the muzzle of her two big guns almost met the one protruding from the Merrimac's port. As the vessels touched there was a shock, a cloud of smoke, a double or treble report. One side of the Monitor's low freeboard slid up the inclined unshakable wall of the Merrimac, the other sank so suddenly that the water curled over and broke upon her deck—the white line of surf extending from stem to stern. As the Monitor recoiled and slid off, she reeled from side to side, unable to fire again, and the Merrimac poured in a full broadside.

"A brave shot," applauded the General. "A few

more like that, Monsieur Ericsson, and your pretty toy will be at the bottom of the sea. Ha! She is turning in shore. She is damaged. She is going to give up the fight." He drew a deep breath, following the Monitor as she drew off into shoal water.

The Merrimac turned slowly, and pointing her prow in the direction of the grounded Minnesota, steamed away, leaving the Monitor, as she believed, in a crippled state. Von Benzinger shut his glasses, put them back in the case, and went slowly down the stairs. His hour of triumph had come. The disabled Monitor could not hope to save the remaining ships in the harbor. Before the sun went down, the Roads would be cleared of every Union vessel, and tomorrow, with the help of the land forces, the Merrimac would take Fortress Monroe. The South, commanding the outlet to the sea from Richmond, and the cork of the bottle being transferred from the James River to the Potomac, recognition by the European powers would follow swiftly. Already he felt upon his brow the victor's crown, already rang in his ears the plaudits of the world.

As he passed along the hall he hesitated, looking toward the door that led to Virginia's room. He saw her again as she stood on the gallery last night, the soft moonlight on her hair and in her eyes. How beautiful she was! He made a step in the direction of her door. Then a low voice, full of pathos, of love, of worship, fell on his ears. It was Black Mammie, praying for her mistress. He stopped. Something of the same feeling took possession of him that he felt in the morning at mention of the dining-room. It was there the courtmartial had been held, and he had caught sight of her white face, as the surgeon carried her by him to the hall. He shrugged his shoulders, and turned to descend the stairs.

"Why should I think of her?" he said, with a proud lifting of his head. "There will be beautiful women, many beautiful women, ready to smile on me tomorrow. The Monitor is beaten, she cannot harm me. Let the girl go to her sailor lover."

As if in answer to his words, there came once more the thunder of that awful gun. It was so sudden, so unexpected, so opposed to all he had been thinking, that it whirled him about as though he had been caught in a cyclone. And before he recovered from the shock, before his dazed brain could realize the overthrow of all his dreams, the report came again, full, forceful, terrible.

Down the stairs he tramped, stepping as though

his feet were shod with lead. In the hall he met Geary, flushed, elated.

"I thought the Monitor was whipped," he stammered.

"So did we all," cried Geary, mistaking the General's excitement for solicitude for the Ericsson ship. "But it was a mistake. Hear her pounding away there? That doesn't sound like defeat, eh? Her commander, Worden, is wounded. They pulled into shoal water, thinking to send him ashore, but he wouldn't leave the ship. They have signaled that he is not dangerously hurt. Lieutenant Greene has taken command, and they have returned to the fight, with unwonted fierceness. That man Hamilton must be all right. The way the Monitor skims around her adversary, pounding her side, firing at her guns, cutting down her flags, knocking over her smokestacks, and getting away before the hippopotamus can harm her, is glorious. Damn me, if I ever saw anything like it."

"Hamilton! Shooting spitballs at a hippopotamus!" The scene of yesterday swept before the eyes of General von Benzinger, distinct, clear, reproachful. Why had he waited? A note to General Wool and all this might have been averted. But the glamour of Waverley was over everything. For the sake of a few hours' conversation with a simple country girl, he had left the scene of action, delayed sending the charges, and now exposure, defeat, death! And a moment ago the prize was almost within his grasp—the cup of glory was at his lips. This man Hamilton had dashed it aside. Bitter, bitter. But there was yet a game to play. He need not fail utterly. If he could hold his present place, other chances would come. These two beings were in his way, but what were they after all? He had the power to crush them. Had not the courtmartial condemned them? Only one thing was lacking, the signature of General Wool. Where was Edwards?

These thoughts whirled through his brain and made him dizzy. He staggered, and Geary, thinking him about to fall, hastily poured out a glass of spirits and offered it to him. He put it on the table untouched. Action! He felt the need of action— air and motion. How those guns roared in his ears. He had heard them all the time, unconsciously noted the increasing ratio of the Monitor's firing to that of the Merrimac's.

"Messengers!" he shouted, suddenly. "Are there no messengers arriving? Are there no dispatches?"

"They have been coming regularly, sir," replied the adjutant.

"Send every man in quarters to the Roads, and

let them bring messages. We must know how the battle goes. Do you hear, Geary? More messengers to the Roads!"

The adjutant went out, and in a few minutes twenty extra men were galloping along the shell road to the shore.

When returning to the house, Geary came upon Estelle. She approached him timidly, and asked him for a pass to ride beyond the gates. The guards had turned her back a few moments before. The Captain tore a leaf from his notebook, and hastily wrote the necessary order. Estelle thanked him, ran to the stables, mounted Bay Nellie, and galloped away. She had gathered from the conversation of Mrs. Poynter and the Squire that General Wool had the power to release Virginia, and she had determined to go to him and tell of her affair with Lafe, and of his taking from her one of Virginia's pistols. While she sincerely mourned the death of Harlan, she was too well aware of Virginia's many virtues to believe her guilty of his death. She felt that somewhere there had been a mistake. Not being able to find the other pistol, she intuitively connected the loss with the tragedy. This much, at least, she could tell to Wool, and she had determined to do so.

During Geary's absence Von Benzinger paced

16

the room like a caged beast. And it was for this he had toiled, and schemed and planned. For this he had sold his honor, sacrificed his manhood, trailed the name of innocence in the dust. How the guns of the Monitor roared. What a voice for Richmond, for Washington, for Paris, for the world! A voice, proclaiming his defeat, his failure, his shame! Messengers came bringing dispatches which he tore into shreds as he read them—always they told the same story—the defeat of the Merrimac. The guns told it, those on the Merrimac growing steadily less, those of the Monitor, steady, constant, fulfilling their destiny. Would it never end? Let the Merrimac go down at once. Utter and final defeat rather than this fine-drawn torture.

Then the sudden resolution to snatch victory from defeat, to shut out all natural feeling, kill every instinct of mercy, to crush and trample on everything; all, rather than go shamefaced against the world. His one ambition had been slain. Let it go. In other fields he would yet succeed. The Merrimac gone, the war would be prolonged. The country was on the threshold of a great struggle. His hand was on the latch of the door that opened to promotion. McClellan was in disfavor at the Capitol. Changes would be sudden and sweeping. The field of battle offered new glories, new triumphs.

Perhaps in the end he might be commander of all the great armies of the North. The new thought dazzled him. The overpowering egotism of the man conquered, and reason ruled again. One thing he lacked to make his position again secure—the approval of General Wool to the findings of the court. If that came his course was decided. The woman should die.

When Geary returned, the General sat at the table, idly drumming on the papers that lay open before him.

"Is there any hope, Geary?" he said, in a hollow voice.

"Hope, General! Of what are you thinking? There's nothing but hope. The guns tell that. The Monitor is firing twice to the. Merrimac's once. She won't have a gun to bear in half an hour. Ericsson is a hero."

Ericsson! Von Benzinger started as though the name had been a nettle, and stung him.

"The messengers, Geary?"

"They have been reinforced, according to your instructions. Those previously posted have been arriving regularly."

The roar of the Monitor's gun, a single shot of the Merrimac, and an orderly stepped into the room, saluting.

"Your message," cried the General. His fingers trembled as he took the paper. "Merrimac drifting helplessly," he read, and the paper slipped from his fingers to the floor.

The sound of hoofs, the clatter of a sword, the hurried tramp of feet, and Edwards entered. General von Benzinger sprang up.

"The papers from General Wool," said Edwards.

As the General reached out his hand and took the document, a great shout went up from the soldiers. In volume it resembled distant thunder. And through it all, an exultant voice, "The Merrimac is whipped. She's running away to Norfolk. Hurrah for the Monitor." The thunder deepened and swelled anew.

General von Benzinger's face darkened at the sound. Then he broke the seal of the document in his hand, and shook it out to its full length. Across the bottom in large black characters was written, "Approved by General Wool."

White as the paper, Von Benzinger stood for a moment, hesitating. Then he lifted the glass of spirits from the table, straightened his shoulders, turned to the Captain, and said, with the old ring in his voice:

"Long live the Union, Captain Geary!"

CHAPTER XVIII.

MARTIAL LAW.

"Long live the Union!" The words were Virginia's real death sentence. The formal sentence of the courtmartial had been merely provisional—having effect only if Von Benzinger decided to remain a Federal. Now he had decided. He set down the empty glass and gazed into it with eyes that saw a thing not really there. Through the soldiers' cheers outside came the notes of mess-call. It was noon. The Monitor was far across the Roads, near the mouth of the Elizabeth, where she had followed her defeated foe.

"It must be done, Captain Geary," said Von Benzinger. "Justice must be done."

"You mean—the prisoner?" asked Geary, his face clouding.

Von Benzinger laid his hand on the findings of the courtmartial. "They are approved by General Wool," he said. "The trial being in the field, during military and naval operations, they do not go to Washington." Noting Geary's expression, he added, "It is a sad and terrible duty, Captain, but a soldier cannot flinch."

"A soldier should not have to do a thing like this!" cried Geary.

"Ah, Geary, that girl's beauty conceals a tiger's heart," replied Von Benzinger, with simulated melancholy. "Think of her influencing her lover to corrupt the pilots. Think of her really murdering the dead heroes of the Cumberland and Congress. Think of her shooting Harlan in cold blood so Hamilton could wreck the Monitor. A man would shrink from such deeds. Why, then, should her sex spare her?"

"It shouldn't, of course," admitted Geary. "She must die, she deserves to die. But a woman—ugh! If it could only be done some other way—not in the usual way!"

"I greatly wish it could!" exclaimed Von Benzinger, sincerely. "If she could lie down and open a vein and sink away quietly—without causing comment—how much better, how much better! But she would not do it herself—foolish religious notions, you know; and the man who would do it for her would be, not her executioner, but her murderer. It must be done as the law prescribes. For her sex the law makes no distinction." The General paced up and down, steeling himself against the human nature that cried out to him to turn back from this legal murder. He could not turn back. There was no way he could prevent the execution of Virginia Eggleston save by confessing his own guilt. Even if he refused to carry out the sentence of the courtmartial, it would be carried out by Colonel Middleton, the next in rank. But he could not confess, he would not refuse to carry out the sentence. "Come, come," he exclaimed, stopping in his walk. "You and I are not killing the girl, Geary, but martial law. The law must be obeyed. Whom do you suggest to conduct the execution?"

"I should hate to suggest anyone," said Geary.

"Did not Stanhope—that Captain in the Sixty-fourth—say he had a brother on the Congress?"

"His brother was there," answered Geary.

"He was killed after the ship was run aground?"

"He was."

"Captain Stanhope shall conduct the execution of his brother's murderess," said the General. "Let it be in the north corner of the grounds. Inform Stanhope. Explain why he is chosen. Let him report here immediately with his company and another, both under his command. Let him station one platoon at the negro quarters, another at the main gate. Place another in open order along the front wall. Place a squad between the house and the appointed spot. Let no one approach. For the firing squad, let him pick out men who obey orders." Von Benzinger paused a moment after rushing through these orders. "And, Geary. As my adjutant, it is your duty to read to the prisoner the decision and the sentence of the court."

Geary turned pale and was about to protest.

"That is all, Geary," said Von Benzinger, cutting him short. "The execution will proceed at once."

The Captain saluted and turned to go.

"Do not forget the document, Captain Geary," said Von Benzinger. "You will find what you want on the last page and a half."

The Captain took up the official paper and went to his room, with a heavy heart. It was right, he felt, but it was horrible. He wrote the order to Captain Stanhope and dispatched an orderly. He took up the findings of the court and turned to that reiterated "guilty" of the summing up. Silently he read the sentence, the signatures of the court and of the Generals commanding. The soldier shuddered—braced himself—and stood up.

Von Benzinger, left alone in his room, sat down,

stood up, paced back and forth, sat down again. He saw Geary pass through the hall and heard him go up the stairs. He heard him speak to the sentry, the sentry's reply, the knock, and the girl's answer. Then she said something to Geary—the voice was gentle and clear, but Von Benzinger could not make out the words. He heard Geary mumble something, and then his voice, reading unsteadily. Von Benzinger knew those words. The recurring "guilty," "guilty," "guilty," came to his ears like the tolling of a bell. The voice went on through charge and sentence to the end—"approved by General Wool." Then came silence—absolute silence.

"Would she not speak?" wondered Von Benzinger—"would she not cry out, or sob, or scream? Why must Geary leave open that door up there?" Von Benzinger made a violent movement and pushed his own door shut. It slammed, and the noise made him start. The door being shut, he wondered if that terrible silence up stairs were still unbroken. He turned the knob, made an opening of an inch or two, and listened. Then her door closed softly, as men close the doors of chambers where the dead lie. Geary tiptoed down the stairs. Von Benzinger shut his door and heard Geary enter his own room.

"Can I endure this?" groaned Von Benzinger.

The better side of his nature—the side he kept chained down because it hampered him and tried to hold him from his purpose—rose in revolt against him. Should he now postpone the execution till tomorrow? Should he steal off tonight to the Confederates, and send back word that Virginia Eggleston was innocent? Yes, and then the world would know that he, Hugo von Benzinger, was a traitor—that he had bribed pilots, grounded ships, accused the innocent, and to shield himself had only failed to murder a helpless woman because his will was weak. Had his ship won, the South would have given him rich rewards, and high command, and no one need have known that he had done worse than offer his plans to the South because the North refused them. His success would have blinded men to the dubious means by which he had achieved it. But now his ship was reported to be in a sinking condition, the Confederates owed him nothing—their disappointment today was as great as their high hopes of yesterday. And when the black schemes of the last twelve hours came out, as out they must, should he confess, the Southerners would despise him. Here he was safe. Here he had honor still and a chance to retrieve past failure. And who was to blame for that failure? Why, she, up stairs, who, with hidden scorn, had fanned his vanity, and wormed his secret out, and turned it against him. She who was, therefore, suffering in her mind the pangs of approaching death. She who loved Hamilton—Hamilton, who had helped to overthrow the power of the Merrimac. Should he release from his grasp and make happy that favored lover—that skillful pilot—that man who had beaten him so far in love and war? No, they deserved to die, and die they should, and they being dead, he would be safe.

Someone was entering the hall, asking the house servant for Mrs. Poynter. Presently the widow came down stairs. Von Benzinger opened his door quietly after she had passed through the hall. Geary's door was closed.

"Oh, Squire!" he heard her say, "did you see Hamilton, did you tell him our awful trouble—what did he do?"

"I saw him, Mrs. Poynter," answered the Squire, in a hopeless voice. "I told him everything. Mr. Willis was there, too?"

"Where?" demanded the widow.

"On the Monitor. Mr. Willis said he shot Harlan."

"Willis? Willis shot Harlan! I knew Virginia didn't do it—even accidentally."

"Willis!" exclaimed Von Benzinger to himself.

His alarm was but momentary. "Pshaw! he cannot read the cipher," he thought.

"Mr. Willis had dispatches of Von Benzinger," went on Henderson.

"S'sh!" warned Mrs. Poynter, and for a few moments Von Benzinger could not catch the Squire's sentence. Then came an exclamation from Mrs. Poynter.

"Struck Willis! Was he killed?"

"It struck his boat, anyhow, Mrs. Poynter. I was too far to see, but I'm afraid he's killed, Mrs. Poynter, I'm afraid he's killed."

There was a rustling of skirts and a little choking sound.

"Earl was just wild when he saw Willis sink," went on Henderson; "he was just wild. He was taking off his things to jump overboard and swim ashore."

"Squire Henderson!" exclaimed Mrs. Poynter. "Why didn't you go back after him?"

There was an uneasy pause, the General smiled grimly as he pictured the flying shells. "It wa'n't no use, Mrs. Poynter. I would 'a gone back, but an officer pointed a pistol at Hamilton an' made him stay!"

"I don't believe it!" cried Mrs. Poynter. She burst into a tirade of abuse, which Von Benzinger was not interested in, and he quietly closed his door. The Squire went on to tell how he had landed and gone back along the shore, but had seen no sign of Willis; how he had gone to the fort, but failed to secure an audience with Wool.

Von Benzinger chuckled with satisfaction. He must avoid Mrs. Poynter, or she would deluge him with this new evidence of Virginia's innocence— evidence which, thanks to the Merrimac's lucky shot, was at the bottom of Hampton Roads. "The iron dragon's dead," mused Von Benzinger, "but still my star is strong—my star is strong." What luck, what superb luck, that the man who killed Harlan was out of the way. And that cipher, too— of course, they could not have read it, but, now, doubtless, it had gone down with Willis, and it was much better to have eighteen feet of salt water over it. And Hamilton's attempt at desertion! That settles Monsieur Hamilton. Nothing could resist such luck as his, combined with such skill. The war would be long, now that the Merrimac was gone, and he might rise to the command of all the forces of the North.

Someone knocked. Was it Mrs. Poynter? How should he get rid of her?

"Come!" he called.

It was Geary. He looked like a sick man.

"There is one thing, General," he said, "ought I not to inform Mrs. Poynter? She is now in the sitting room."

"No, no, no," answered Von Benzinger, impatiently, "she will cry, she will talk. Refuse her admittance to me. Tell her I'm busy. Put her off. It will soon be too late to talk. Thank fortune that the other has so far kept still."

"I will never forget Virginia Eggleston's look," said Geary, solemnly, "never to my dying day. It was worse than ten thousand words—the most heart-breaking look I ever saw on a human face."

"You must keep your mind from brooding on this subject, Captain Geary," replied Von Benzinger. "Remember her crimes."

"I cannot, I cannot," answered Geary.

His emotion troubled Von Benzinger, who could not, with all his will-power, quench the unwelcome pity and remorse that rose within him. She was so mute, so helpless. If she had only accused him, denounced him, hurled invectives at him, he could have gloried in her overthrow. If only Hamilton were there with her to struggle and suffer man-fashion, not in this heart-breaking silence. But after the battle they would take Hamilton from the Monitor and put him in irons.

There was a knock at the door. It was an orderly announcing Captain Stanhope. The Captain entered. He was a tall, grave man, who carried his hat in his hand and bowed stiffly.

"General von Benzinger," he said, "I have brought my company and another. I have not yet disposed them according to your orders. Before I do so, I wish to say that I have never flinched from my duty as a soldier, but I beg you will choose someone else for this. My brother died for his country. No doubt the courtmartial is right. The woman to be shot must have committed the dreadful crime which cost so many lives. But she is now to suffer, not our vengeance, but our justice. And the assignment of this duty to me adds to the execution the element of revenge. Again, sir, I respectfully request to be relieved."

"Because you do not flinch from a disagreeable duty, sir," replied Von Benzinger, "you are the man for this. Your idea of justice is very correct. Having that idea, it is just that you should do this thing. You have no choice in the matter, therefore you have no responsibility. You will carry out your instructions at once, Captain Stanhope. Captain Geary will show you the documents, by authority of which I give you this order."

Captain Stanhope examined the findings, returned to his command, and disposed his men about the grounds, according to Von Benzinger's orders. The soldiers off duty in the near-by regiments got wind that something of importance was about to happen at headquarters, and in the woods between the house and the river they came as close as the numerous guards would let them. The guards had orders to let no one enter the grounds or linger on the road outside until the execution was over.

It was half-past twelve.

The Monitor was dropping anchor by the Minnesota.

CHAPTER XIX.

JUSTICE.

The sergeant of the firing squad had loaded twelve pieces. Some contained powder and ball, others powder only. No man would know whether the pressure of his trigger had contributed to the death of the prisoner. The men of the squad filed past the sergeant, who handed each one a musket. They then fell in and the sergeant marched them to their place. This was two hundred paces behind the house, on the side of the grounds away from the negro cabins and the stables. They faced, at fifteen paces, the white stone wall which separated the enclosure about the house from the open fields behind it. To their left ran a stake and rider rail fence, of which the angles were full of wild shrubs and vines. Beyond the fence were noble woods, deep in which were the Union outposts. Fruit trees screened the spot from the view of the passers on the Newport

17

road.   Only from the front gate itself could the place be seen, and the guard there would allow no one to stop an instant.   A grapevine arbor and oak trees cut off the view of the house from the angle of the rail fence and the stone wall where the prisoner was to stand.   The long, blue-grass in that corner was dustless, fresh and sweet.

The squad waited.   Captain Stanhope was the only officer present.   The Chaplain was with the prisoner.   When she had prayed with him, then she would come.

From the house came a woman's wail of anguish that made men stop their ears.   The cry was re-echoed from the cabins where the negroes huddled, terrified by the platoon drawn up in front of them, and the dreadful preparation going on.   The house door opened.   Two soldiers stepped out.   Then came Virginia, deathly pale and dressed in black; behind her, two more soldiers, then the Chaplain and Surgeon Cuthbertson.   In wild agitation Mrs. Poynter and Henderson followed, but were stopped by the guard outside, and ordered back into the house.   Virginia stopped between the soldiers and looked back.

"Good-bye, Cora," she said.

Again that cry rang out, and Mrs. Poynter fell insensible on the gallery floor.   The Squire bent

over her, the tears streaming down his cheeks.
A choking sob shook Virginia as she turned away,
but her eyes fell on the waiting squad, and the white
wall where she would stand, and the grass where
she would fall, quiet at last, with no more pain.
The infinite calmness of death swept through her
mind, soothing and strengthening. This thing was
certain, immediate—there was no more hope to
torture her—no hope of Willis nor of Earl. If they
came, they would come too late. Firmly she walked
to the appointed place, and stood with bowed head,
waiting. In the black dress her figure was clearly
marked against the white wall. A big soldier in
the squad looked at her and thought. He grew
dizzy, and fell like a log. His musket clattered on
the ground; two men fell out and carried him over
near the rail fence. The big man had caused delay.

Someone near was clumsily preparing a bandage
for her eyes—perhaps it was Major Cuthbertson.

"Oh, please be quick," she said. "I cannot bear
it long."

What was that stir at the front gate? Virginia
looked up. Through the one break in the trees
she caught sight of a man on horseback. Her heart
gave a great leap. Was it reprieve? Was it Earl?
The man was hatless and coatless. He spoke to
the guard in front of the closed gates, the guard

shook his head and brought his bayonet to the charge. The man said something else, the guard hesitated, came to port arms and called the corporal. Oh, bitterness! The man was going away; he had turned his horse off into the woods. No, he was dashing back—across the road—horse and rider rose over the wall—they had cleared it—no, the spikes struck the animal's hind legs—horse and rider rolled on the ground, the horse could not rise. But the man was up and was running toward the house. Henderson was calling and motioning to him, pointing in her direction. Two or three guards at the house stood in his path, with their bayonets ready. Everyone near Virginia turned, expecting to see the man halted by these guards. But the man said something to them, which made them hesitate an instant, and in that instant the man dashed past, and came straight on, running toward her, toward her. It was Earl, it was Earl, and Virginia, calling out his name in a great cry of joy, sprang toward him, and before the men about her could prevent, she was clasped in his powerful arms, and felt that she would not die. Men threw themselves upon him, but he pushed them off. "Wait!" he exclaimed. "The execution must stop! The woman is innocent!" The men heard authority in the voice, fell back a little, and looked at Captain Stanhope.

"By whose order do you come here?" asked the Captain. "Who are you?"

"I am Hamilton, Lieutenant, United States Navy. I know this woman is innocent."

"Do you say this upon your own responsibility? Have you nothing from the proper authorities to prevent this execution?"

"Good God, man," exclaimed Hamilton. "Had I waited to see the proper authorities, where would the girl be now?"

"I cannot disobey my instructions upon so flimsy an argument as this," said Captain Stanhope, rigidly. "How do I know you are a Lieutenant in the Navy?"

"Because I tell you so," flashed Hamilton, who was not used to having men doubt his word.

"Well, suppose you are? What authority has a Lieutenant in the Navy to interrupt a military execution?"

"I tell you, because the woman is innocent."

"You have no authority to tell me anything, and I have none to listen to you," replied Stanhope. "The execution will proceed."

"The execution will *not* proceed," came the answer, so quick, so decisive, that the soldiers stood staring, not knowing what to do. This unarmed man, whose face was black with burned powder, who wore no insignia of rank upon his person, had by sheer will power broken the strong bonds of military discipline. The twelve soldiers whose orders were to shoot the prisoner became a jury before which Hamilton had secured for her a new trial.

"So this is Lieutenant Hamilton!" The group of men started and turned toward the new—the mocking voice. It was Von Benzinger, who stood coolly eyeing the powerful sailor. He had been waiting in his room for the sound of the volley which should send the shattering bullets through the beautiful girlish figure he had loved. Not hearing the volley, he came out, and saw that something unexpected was interrupting the execution. Divining the arrival of Hamilton, he hailed it with delight—it meant a struggle—a battle—a victory for him. It was far less revolting—and here were both his enemies together in his power.

"Von Benzinger!" exclaimed Virginia.

At the name, the light of hatred kindled in Hamilton's eyes. A wild impulse seized him to hurl himself upon Von Benzinger and kill him with his weaponless hands. But such a movement would precipitate a dozen armed men upon him, and even could he instantly kill Von Benzinger, how would that help? He himself would probably die the next instant, and leave Virginia to her doom. No, he must win these men, he must convince them of Von Benzinger's guilt. What then? What if he did convince them? He had no tangible proof. A second trial, could he secure it, would bring out nothing new. The desperateness of the situation flashed through his brain in that one meeting with his enemy's cool, well-assured eyes.

"Lieutenant Hamilton," repeated Von Benzinger. "The naval officer who hired Confederate pilots for the fleet."

A stir of indignation started among the men, but Hamilton's fiery answer rang above it—the first words he had ever spoken to Von Benzinger.

"You lie, you hound! You did that thing yourself. And then you put your guilt upon a woman, an innocent woman."

Von Benzinger's words were plausible, Hamilton's incredible, and yet the sailor's voice was not that of a man lying. The big man who had fainted, revived and sat up, listening. The whole squad waited for Von Benzinger's reply.

"The courtmartial, not I, found her guilty," he said. "And, Monsieur Hamilton, the same courtmartial recommended your immediate arrest and trial for treason. The woman is but your accomplice. Is that so, Major Cuthbertson?"

"It is," replied the surgeon.

Von Benzinger's case was almost won. At that moment the men would have obeyed the order to shoot Hamilton down.

"Yes, your courtmartial said so," answered Hamilton. "They acted on such evidence as the note you forged—the note from Buchanan to me. That forgery did not reach its destination, but you could easily make others."

"Who had that note?" asked Von Benzinger. Then he added quickly—"which was not forged."

"Waterloo Willis, of the secret service, shot Harlan and took from him the cipher you sent Buchanan. In it, you remember, you told the Merrimac's Captain to board and lash the Monitor, cover her turret with tarpaulins and throw in hand grenades." The stir of indignation veered and turned against Von Benzinger. Major Cuthbertson looked surprised.

For an instant, only, Von Benzinger looked anxious. Then he laughed. "Waterloo Willis," he repeated. "Did he take with him this queer dispatch of mine to the bottom of Hampton Roads? It is very easy to say what papers were in *his* pockets—but who believes such tales?" Von Benzinger gloated over Hamilton's expression of discomfiture. Earl still had a lingering hope that Willis had escaped. Had this omniscient schemer not known of Willis' death, the sudden revelation of the cipher's interpretation would have shaken him badly.

"Unfortunately for you, General von Benzinger," said Earl, in desperation, "Willis gave me that dispatch before his boat was sunk."

For an instant Von Benzinger quailed. The jury, watching him, swung clear over to Hamilton's side. But Von Benzinger had noted the subtle note of falsehood in the sailor's voice. Quick as a flash he staked his game upon that chance. "Where is it, then?" he said, defiantly. Earl did not think he would have courage to say that.

"It is not here," he was forced to answer, and instantly he lost far more than he had gained.

Von Benzinger pressed his advantage. "What monstrosities you speak!" he exclaimed. "That you possess such a paper and do not bring it here is incredible—childish!" He saw that the iron was hot. "Captain Stanhope," he said—

"Soldiers of the North!" It was Virginia who spoke. "This man, your General, made iron ships in France. Is that not true?"

"What of it?" said Von Benzinger, impatiently.

Cuthbertson knew of it, therefore it could not be denied.

"He offered to the North plans for a Merrimac—the North refused. Therefore, he built the Merrimac for the South. Therefore, he bribed the pilots to run the ships aground. Last night, when his ship was victorious, he told me all, because I was a Confederate. When the Monitor came he plotted to accuse her pilot, Hamilton, so the Merrimac might win. Confederate though I am, I tried to warn that pilot, and for that I am to die. I did not plot to ground the ships. I did not kill Harlan. I knew that General von Benzinger was a traitor, and that knowledge is my only crime." These clear and solemn words came to the men like perfect truth. Ah, why could Virginia not have spoken when alone in that courtmartial as she spoke now in helping Earl?

"Willis killed Harlan," put in Hamilton. "He killed him because Harlan was plotting with Von Benzinger to accuse me and so leave the Monitor without a pilot. Willis took from Harlan, Von Benzinger's treasonable cipher to the Merrimac."

"The courtmartial decided that Virginia Eggleston killed Harlan," said Von Benzinger, cold and strong. "She took from him my dispatch accusing you. Had not that been done, you would be now in irons." Von Benzinger determined to end the strange scene with which he had been merely amusing himself. "How do you account for the fact, Lieutenant Hamilton, that, just before the battle, you tried to swim ashore from the Monitor and were forced, with leveled pistol, to remain and pilot her?"

"Because, for an instant, when I heard that you were foully murdering this innocent girl, I determined to come here at any cost and save her. I did *not* leave my ship—I suffered the tortures of the damned—I piloted the Monitor, and all men could see if it was a traitor's piloting."

"A pistol muzzle is sometimes an excellent antidote for treason," sneered Von Benzinger. "Often a musket is equally effective. Captain Stanhope, we will try a little of this medicine. Proceed with your duty.'" The swift and bitter argument for Virginia's life had been a drawn battle. To overcome the soldiers' discipline, Hamilton knew that he required a complete victory. He knew now that the soldiers would obey their officers.

"Sergeant!" called Stanhope. Listening to the debate, the squad had lost its formation. No one was in his proper place. The Captain turned to look for his sergeant. Suddenly he felt his sword fly from its scabbard, and caught at it—too late. Hamilton had it, and recovering from his rush, the Lieutenant turned toward Von Benzinger—desperate, all hope gone, but determined that this man should die.

"Shoot him!" cried Von Benzinger, at the same time drawing his sword. One of the soldiers obeyed. He quickly raised his piece, covered Hamilton, who was at that instant motionless, not ten feet away—and fired. There was a roar—a puff of red-lit smoke, enveloping the Lieutenant, and the men waited to see him fall. But out of the smoke he sprang—the powder had burned his clothing. The charge in that piece was blank. With fury he rushed upon Von Benzinger—the two were so close no man could fire. Von Benzinger was an expert and fearless swordsman, but he knew Hamilton had the advantage of utter desperation. Therefore he had called upon the soldiers to shoot; therefore, when the shot was vain, he stood to his guard with utmost wariness. The sailor would have had an advantage in his prodigious length of arm, but he was not upon the defensive. Using the merely decorative officer's sword as a cutlass, he hurled his body straight upon his enemy's, sweeping his sword aside as he came. Had he missed, he would himself have been impaled. The stroke snapped his own blade a foot from the hilt, at the point where the two swords met. Hamilton's left arm clinched Von Benzinger, and they came breast to breast. Von Benzinger's right hand shot far back of him, shortening his sword and trying to bring his point against Hamilton's body. Hamilton did the same, but he had to recover from the stroke which, sweeping Von Benzinger's sword to the right, had carried his own far to the left. Von Benzinger's thrust came first, while Hamilton was drawing back his hand. As the blow started, Hamilton bent to the right, pressed his left elbow out against Von Benzinger's sword arm, and so changed the course of the point that it merely grazed the skin. With terrific force Hamilton plunged his broken blade clean to the hilt in Von Benzinger's body. The General gave one gasp, the life went out of his limbs, and, as he sank down, Hamilton wrenched out his sword. Von Benzinger fell face down, and his gleaming hair lay in the dustless blue-grass.

For a moment no one spoke or stirred. The whole thing—the snatching of the sword, the musket shot, the miracle of Hamilton's escape, the cutlass stroke and the deadly thrust, had been the matter of a very few seconds.

The surgeon's instinct was the first to produce action. Major Cuthbertson, who had come here expecting to pronounce Virginia's life extinct, knelt by Von Benzinger, and looked at the location of the wound. One look sufficed.

The sergeant, recovering his wits, snatched up a musket, determined that there should be no more trifling with this naval man.

"Wait!" commanded Captain Stanhope. The sergeant stopped.

"Major Cuthbertson," said Stanhope. "Is there anything we can do?"

"General von Benzinger is dead," replied Cuthbertson.

"Lieutenant Hamilton," said Stanhope. "Whatever be the truth of this matter, I place you under arrest on the charge of murder. Will you submit, or shall my men use force? There are some guns here with bullets in them."

"Captain Stanhope," answered Earl, "you may riddle me with bullets, but I will not stand by and see this woman shot."

"Captain Stanhope," said Major Cuthbertson, "I have no power to countermand your orders, but this whole scene has convinced me that there is a side of this wretched business which is not yet known. If Lieutenant Hamilton will submit to arrest and trial, you can well afford to await further orders before you shoot the girl."

"Do you agree to this, Lieutenant Hamilton?" asked the Captain.

"It is all that I have fought for," answered Earl.

"Is General Wool in?" The questioner was hatless and coatless.

CHAPTER XX.

SECRET SERVICE.

"Is General Wool in?" The questioner was hatless and coatless. His blue shirt and gray trousers were grimy and dusty. The trim orderly could not repress a look of amused scorn as he ran his eye slowly from the man's soiled boots to his uncombed hair.

"Did you expect to see him?" There was irony in the voice and attitude of the sentinel. Here was an opportunity to "get even" for past indignities suffered at the hands of his superiors.

"Damn your impudence, yes. Is he in?"

The smart orderly frowned, and drew back his foot, preparatory to kicking the presumptuous civilian down the steps. Before the movement could be executed, the man leaned forward and uttered two words in a low voice. The orderly suddenly resumed an upright attitude, saluted and said, hurriedly:

"I'll inform the General at once, sir."

He returned a moment later and stood at attention, saluted, and said, "You are to go in now, sir."

When the man had disappeared behind the big oaken door, the orderly rubbed his chin thoughtfully and muttered. "What the devil—looks more like a tramp." But the effort of thinking was painful, and he lapsed into his usual attitude, staring stonily into the street.

Five, ten, twenty minutes went by. Officers of high rank came into the hall, their swords clicking musically on the stone steps, to receive the information the General was engaged and could not be seen. An hour later, the door opened and the man came out again, in a somewhat more presentable shape than when he went in. Now, he wore a hat, and a revolver was in his belt. Over his shoulder was slung a leathern pouch used by messengers to carry dispatches. General Wool accompanied him to the door.

"I trust you'll be in time," he said, with great earnestness. "We were fortunate in reaching Stanton at once. The wires are not always so accommodating. Have you a good horse?"

"The best in Virginia, I'm told."

"Will you require an escort?"

"No, sir. That would detain me. I'll ride alone. Good-bye."

He ran down the steps, sprang into the saddle, and galloped away. The horse, a bright bay, swept over the ground with a long, regular stride, going easily, smoothly, swiftly as a swallow flies. Long of body, deep of chest, narrow of flank, with slender, but beautifully shaped legs, there was a noticeable harmony between horse and rider. The same hint of suppressed force in the square, lean shoulders, the clean limbs, the long, big-veined neck reaching forward eagerly. The man stroked the mare's black, glossy mane, speaking words of encouragement.

"Steady, old girl. It's a good eight-mile brush, and you musn't fail. Remember, it is for her, your mistress—Virginia."

The mare tossed her head, as if she understood, and went forward at an increased pace. Down the long driveway, skirting the shore, past white houses, half hidden in running vines, by green lawns, under spreading shade trees, through the straight streets of military camps, by Newport News, over the sand dunes, splashing through the ford, and then—the red turrets of Waverley.

"By Jimtown!" cried the rider, suddenly pulling up the mare at the timber's edge, "may I never see New England again, if that isn't Estelle and the

Squire's nigger Joe. Must be something wrong. I sent her back to Waverley two hours ago. What is it, girl?" he cried, leaping to the ground. "Von Benzinger up to any new devilment?"

"Hamilton!" exclaimed Estelle, greatly excited.

"Arrested, I suppose. Don't let that worry you, I've seen Wool. Hamilton's all right."

"You don't know. He went straight from the boat to Waverley, found them preparing to shoot Virginia, and he—"

"Killed Von Benzinger. Of course. And Virginia?"

"The officer who heard Hamilton's story had them both locked up. They are going to have another investigation. It all happened just before I got back after giving you Bay Nellie. Seth told me about it."

"Von Benzinger! And so the old schemer is beyond doing any more harm in this world," drawled Willis, shaking himself into his old-time, easy ways. "Well, that makes further haste unnecessary on our part, Nellie." The correspondent patted the mare. "Is Captain Geary there?" he said, again addressing Estelle.

"Yes, sir. I saw him crossing the yard as I came away? Oh, Mr. Willis, do you think Miss Virginia will forgive me? I brought all this on her. She nevah killed Lafe, I knew she didn't. He took her pistol from me."

"Nobody believes her guilty," said Willis, cheerfully. "I've got Stanton's order for her release right here. Harlan—well, he fell in a fair fight. By Jimtown! you shall carry this bit of precious paper to Miss Eggleston yourself. That'll even matters. I've got to hunt up Colonel Middleton, he's next in command after Von Benzinger, and get Hamilton off."

"And am I really to take the pardon to Virginia?" cried the girl, beaming with delight at the prospect.

"Surely.· Oh, I say, where'd you run across the Squire's property? He was lost about a year ago I remember."

"Yesterday," corrected Estelle.

"So it was. Seem's longer. Where was he?"

"I found him leading a horse down here to water just before you came. I turned the horse loose and am going to fetch Joe to the Squire."

"Good. Here's a note to Hamilton, too. I suppose he thinks I'm out there at the bottom of the pond. There, that'll ease his mind and let him know I'm after orders for his release. Run along now, messenger of mercy! Give the papers to Geary and tell him I said you were to deliver them in person."

"Oh, Mr. Willis!"

"Run along; whoa, Nellie—no, you can't go home just yet."

The correspondent splashed back through the ford and disappeared over the rise. And up the slope to Waverley, hand in hand, went the two young slaves, the articulate and the dumb, bearing the message of freedom.

*   *   *   *   *   *   *

The sun was casting long shadows on the lawn at Waverley, when Willis rode into the grounds, and called cheerily to Geary, pacing up and down the gallery. Seth took Bay Nellie to the stables, talking volubly to the tired animal, and giving her many an affectionate stroke with his wrinkled hand. Willis mounted the steps and received the Captain's hearty congratulations with cool indifference.

"Too thin to be struck by a shell and too light to sink, that's all, Captain," he drawled. "Some call it Kismet. How are your prisoners? All right? Good. Thought my news would prove a tonic. Wool was about the most surprised man you ever saw. Entertained me in my shirt sleeves. We kept the wires hot to Washington, and Stanton grasped the situation wonderfully for a man not on the ground. But Hamilton was too quick for me."

"It is fortunate he was," said Geary, significantly, "otherwise you would have come too late."

Willis shuddered. "Don't, Geary," he said. "The thought gives me the horrors. There's Wool's order for Hamilton's release. Where is he?"

"In the library. Lieutenant!" called Geary.

Edwards came and Geary gave the required orders to take the guards out of the house, and also to remove the headquarters to camp. "I can't stay here, Willis."

"I understand, Captain, and respect your feelings. See you later. I must shake hands with Earl."

In the hall he met Estelle, happy in having been readily forgiven. "You might tell Miss Eggleston there's a friend of hers waiting to see her in the library," he said, "and also suggest to Mrs. Poynter that a Washington co'espondent might have a bit of interesting gossip."

A moment later Hamilton and Willis gripped each other's hands, and looked each other in the eyes. What they thought belongs to themselves. Whatever it was, they evidently found words too cheap to tell it. Hamilton threw his long arm over the shoulder of his friend and said, slowly:

"It's all right, old fellow. I'll never forget you, never."

"I wish I had a seegar," said Willis, with more nervousness than he had ever before shown. "Little bit hurried down to the fort, and forgot to lay in a supply."

"The same old Willis," laughed Hamilton. Willis joined him and they both felt better.

"The last time I saw you, Willis," said the Lieutenant, a little later, "I thought you were killed. God!" The memory of that awful moment swept over him, and he turned to the window to hide his emotion.

" 'Twas close," said Willis, feigning to be searching for something along the mantle. "The shell struck the boat nearly in the center, and spoiled it completely. When I came up later, I looked around for a piece of the wreck big enough to keep me afloat, for I'm not exactly a duck in the water— never could learn to swim much. But there wasn't a piece larger than my hand in the whole district. I paddled around as best I could in my soaked clothes and with my boots full of water, but I wouldn't have lasted long had not a merciful wave tossed me a half-burnt spar of the Congress. I managed to tie myself to that with my neckerchief, and then took it as easy as I could. Everybody aboard ship was too intent on the fight to see anything else. It was near high tide, and I was carried about three miles along the shore toward Newport News. Just when I was getting near enough the point to begin to think of landing, the tide turned, and back I went over the same course. The Monitor and Merrimac were fighting close to me several times, but I didn't take any notes of the fight."

"How did you finally get to see Wool? Your note, brought by Estelle, said you'd been to the fort."

"Oh, I got ashore at last somewhere between Newport News and Hampton, but I was so completely played out I couldn't undo the knot in my tie, and might have lain there till this time but for a happy circumstance."

"Did the widow come to your rescue?" laughed Earl.

The correspondent colored slightly, but replied in the same old drawl. "No, Estelle came riding along on Bay Nellie, going to the fort to try and help Virginia. She saw me, released me, gave me the horse, and I sent her back to Waverley to tell them here I was alive. I rode to the fort, water-soaked as I was, and got insulted by an orderly standing guard over Wool. But the General was gracious enough to take me in, muddy boots and all. I showed him the papers about—"

"You little black runaway nigger."

"The Squire and his property, by Jimtown,"

laughed Willis. "I'll conclude the story some other time."

"Ef I evah catch yo' holding the hoss o' one o' these heah Yankee encroachers on the sacred soil o' the Confederacy an' violatin' the constitution, I'll hoss-whip yo' within an inch o' yo' life," came the voice of the Squire.

"Glorious!" cried Willis. "Earl, if I can get the Squire and that boy up to Washington, I'll make the hit of my life."

"I declare, Squire, if you haven't found your property!" cried Mrs. Poynter, descending the steps into the hall.

Hamilton bounded out to her, and seized her hands. "How is Virginia?" he asked, anxiously.

"The good news which that dear angel, Willis, has been showering upon us has braced her up wonderfully," replied Mrs. Poynter. "When she heard of your release, she got up, and she's coming down to see you."

A great wave of thankfulness swept over Hamilton; for, after the terrible experience of that afternoon, he had carried Virginia, unconscious and deathly white, to her room. There Major Cuthbertson had given directions which Black Mammie followed, with tenderest care, and Hamilton had been taken to the library, a prisoner. Now, four hours later, Mrs. Poynter, wishing to let the rescued lovers meet alone, invented an errand for the Squire. The old fellow bowed himself out, and nearly became cross-eyed in his attempt to keep one eye on Mrs. Poynter and the other on Joe. Finally, however, he departed, devoting both eyes and his eloquent tongue to his beloved "property." Then the widow, leaving Hamilton at the foot of the stairs, started to pass through the sitting-room. Seeing Willis, she hesitated a moment, and then held out her hands to him. He came forward, and took them in his own, shook them awkwardly, and then looking questioningly about the room, drawled, "You don't happen to know the whereabout of a seegar, do you, Mrs. Poynter? I forgot to lay in a supply down at the fort."

"Come with me," said the widow, the warm color sweeping into her cheeks. "But you *are* a dear angel, Waterloo, and a great good fellow, and I'm going to tell you so whether you want me to or not."

Half an hour later, Earl and Virginia stepped out upon the gallery. The sun was setting, and the western sky was aglow with delicate shades of gold and amethyst and purple. In the elm tree, down by the gate, a thrush proclaimed his joy. Over near Fort Monroe a pale pillar of smoke rose, slender and straight in the quiet air. It was the Monitor standing guard across the road to Washington.

Virginia, still very weak, leaned upon her lover's arm, and oh, how welcome its support after her lonely anguish! "Think of it, Earl," she said, "it was only yesterday—yesterday noon—that we stood there beneath those trees—and I—" she paused, and the color came to her face.

"And you," he said, "spoke words that echoed in my brain amid the roar of battle. I hear them still—those words—'I love you, Earl'—so sweet, so wonderful that I can scarce believe them now."

"You must have little faith," she said, "if you cannot believe them now."

"I do believe, Virginia. No power on earth can shake my faith, after—after all you've suffered for my sake."

Her pallor came again, and he reproached himself bitterly for bringing to her mind those dreadful memories. But she looked at him and new thoughts came and brought her color back, and then she spoke—her voice like deepest flute-notes, thrilled with love's warmer tones.

"I cannot say I did not suffer. I suffered things almost unbearable—for you, my Earl. But did you not suffer, too—for me? You offered your life for mine; you guarded me with splendid strength, and if you had not come, I would be—not here with you, dear one. But listen—now it is over, now I am here with you, I say it is worth the price. For this—for you I'd bear it all again."

"Dearest Virginia," answered he, "a lifetime's happiness can hardly pay you for these days. The love of all my years is yours, and love is strong. But if I am so blest that I can make you happy all your life, I still shall be your debtor—still have all to pay."

Her steady eyes were looking into his, and in their depths he saw, splendid and holy, a light which was her soul made visible. The glory passed into his heart, the hush of worship came upon him, and he knew that here, shining in a woman's eyes, he beheld what men call God.

EPILOGUE.

UNION.

The Maine had been destroyed in Havana Harbor. North and South had sprung to arms. In Dixie and in Yankeeland scores of regiments were mobilizing to fight, not each other, but a foreign foe. The North Atlantic squadron had drawn its line along the Cuban coast; Dewey, half the world away, had left Mirs Bay to find and destroy the enemy's vessels. The Flying Squadron lay in Hampton Roads, ready to guard our coast or threaten that of Spain.

Commodore Hamilton, retired now from active service, sat late one afternoon in April on the gallery at Waverley, looking down upon the scene of the first great sea fight between iron ships.

Instead of the tents of Camp Butler, rose the roofs of Newport News, where deep-sea freighters came for grain, where locomotives pulled and pushed their cars of coal, and flying electric cars carried tourists to the great hotels, and Hampton, and the fort. Down there on the shore where so long ago fool infantrymen had shot spit-balls at the Hippopotamus, hundreds of men were laying the foundations of the greatest ship-yard in the world. Up at the fort they were planting the disappearing guns, and there was talk of tearing down the great hotels.

Instead of the frigates Minnesota and Roanoke and St. Lawrence, lay the cruiser Brooklyn, with her lofty smokestacks, the great, turreted battle-ships, Texas and Massachusetts, and the low ram, Katahdin. There were the rusted monitors of long ago, manned now by naval militia, and a host of lesser ships—the Sterling, Saturn, Scorpion and Co-lumbia.

A sweet-faced lady with beautiful white hair came out of the house and joined the Commodore.

"Virginia, dear," he said, pointing to one of the smaller vessels, "there is the Merrimac."

"The Merrimac!" exclaimed Mrs. Hamilton, looking around as though she expected to see a phantom ship. "Are you dreaming, dear boy?"

"No. The name which once struck terror to the nation's heart is borne now by yonder inglorious collier—the truckster of the fleet. 'To what base uses may we not descend!' The Merrimac a collier, the monitors full of land lubbers, and I an old hulk here ashore, while the youngsters, Waterloo and Earl Junior, sail off to thrash the Dons."

"Is the haven so unwelcome?" asked the Commodore's wife.

"The best any man ever had," he said, with deep sincerity.

"Two sons who wear the blue should prove *this* rebel reconstructed, Earl."

"They will fight well, Virginia girl. They are your sons."

The lady's face grew solemn as she remembered how their father fought one day long years ago.

The Commodore was eyeing the huge bulk of the Massachusetts.

"The old Merrimac is scrap iron and ashes now," he mused, "beneath the sea, the old Monitor lies on the tie-ribs of earth, where the blind white sea snakes are. But look, Virginia, yonder Massachusetts—a floating iron fortress, turret-crowned—what is she but the Monitor upon the Merrimac—the vessels of the North and South made one?"

THE END.

9 7 8 3 3 3 7 3 4 7 8 0 2